HATTIE

HATTIE

Frida Nilsson

ILLUSTRATIONS BY STINA WIRSÉN

GECKO PRESS

AT HOME
WITH
HATTIE

This is the story of Hattie. She's six years old and about to start school at last.

Her school is in Hardemo. That's a tiny, tiny town in the country. The town is so far out in the middle of nowhere that hardly anyone goes there. Except for Hattie.

She's been waiting forever to start school, to go on the school bus, then run the last bit. She'll never be able to bike to school because she lives far too far away. Hattie doesn't even live in the middle of nowhere. She lives outside it.

Hattie's house is red and called Ängatorp, which means meadow house. Her mother is in the kitchen changing the vacuum cleaner bag. She's tired because she's been working all night at the hospital.

And yet, Hattie thinks, she's never too tired for cleaning. Sometimes she wonders if her mother's lying when she says how boring it is to get out the bucket and mop. Whatever Hattie finds boring she avoids whenever she can. Brushing teeth, eating fish, changing her underwear and going to bed, for example. She particularly avoids cleaning. And she suspects that her mother secretly finds cleaning one of the loveliest things you can do.

Her father is upstairs writing. He's in a hurry. He has an hour before he has to jump into the blue car and zoom to the newspaper office in town to talk about his article. He's a journalist and has sacrificed himself many times for the sake of the news.

Once the newspaper wanted an article on how to survive in the wild without provisions. So her father went out into the forest and caught a magpie with his bare hands! Then he grilled it on an open fire and ate it up. After that he wrote in the newspaper about his experience. The magpie tasted almost like chicken.

The wind sings in the trees around the red house, and sheep bleat in the barn. There are jabbering ducks in the duckhouse, and hens that wander about and poop in her mother's flowerbeds. In the woodshed is a turkey keeping out of the fox's way, and in the basement are a thousand spiders just waiting for a chance to squiggle inside Hattie's top.

Spades and rakes hang in the puppy shed. The puppies went to new homes ages ago; now there's just the old mother left. Her name is Tacka and she's black with white on her tail. She's never bitten a single person. But if Hattie wants to put her on a leash and take her for a nice walk, she runs into the trees and hides for hours. Hattie thinks this is strange. If she was a dog, she'd want to be on the leash all day. The leash is so pretty!

There are also two stripy outdoor cats. Havana and Stick. Havana is nice and cleans herself on Hattie's lap in the evenings. Stick is horrible. He comes into the house when he's hungry, and then Hattie has to run and hide in the bathroom. If there's no food in the cat bowls, Stick tries to eat Hattie instead. He grabs onto her leg, gnawing and biting.

"Mama, feed the cats!" cries Hattie, kicking her leg to shake Stick free. As soon as he hears the rattle of cat food in the kitchen, Stick shoots off like an arrow and Hattie can breathe out.

But then, while Stick sleeps fat and full in front of the heater, Hattie creeps over to the bowls. She takes a few leftover cat biscuits. She creeps behind the living room curtain and eats them up. Her mother would rather she ate beef and dill stew. But Hattie loves cat food. It tastes almost like chips.

This summer Hattie has rummaged around outside every day. In the evenings she's been watching a great show on TV. Hattie is jealous of the main character, Lisa. She has two sisters living next door on one side and a sister and brother on the other. Hattie has no one next door. Only an old man called Alf who drives a digger.

"I'm so booored," she complains.

Her father puts his head to one side. "Little shrimp." He ruffles her hair. Then he says that as soon as school starts she'll never be bored. Hattie is looking forward to it so much she might burst.

THE BLACK BUS

One day, when Hattie is out on the lawn, a black bus comes cruising along the road. It has tinted windows and crawls past the house. Her mother is sitting on the steps planting flowers in pots. She thinks the bus is up to no good. It must be thieves looking for a house to break into!

The bus turns around at the corner and rolls past again. "Run in and get paper and a pen," Mama tells Hattie. "So we can write down the registration number."

Finally, something's happening in the outside of nowhere. Hattie runs into the kitchen and is back in a second with paper and pen.

"Sneak over and write it down," whispers her mother. She is crouching on the porch, squinting at the bus.

Hattie creeps up behind the lilac hedge. At the mailbox she ducks down in the grass and is just about to write down the numbers when the bus stops and the window rolls down! A man with brown curly hair who's chewing tobacco sticks his head out.

Beside the curly-haired man there's another thief, wearing a cap and a leather jacket. Hattie feels terror run through her. She stares, panic-stricken, back at the porch.

Her mother comes running as fast as her clogs can carry her, the sharp garden rake at the ready.

"Are you Hattie?" asks the curly man.

Her mother's mouth opens.

"Yes," squeaks Hattie.

The men are very pleased. They explain that they've been driving around for an hour looking for Hattie's place. They're bus drivers and they drive the bus that will take Hattie to school. Her mother looks surprised but throws the rake in the grass and puts out her hand.

"Good, that's great," she says, smiling.

Then she stands for a long time talking with the bus drivers.

At last the curly one turns to Hattie. "What were you doing with the pen and paper, by the way?"

Just then her mother decides they've talked long enough. She and Hattie must go in at once and make lunch. The men surely have to be on their way.

Hattie stands in the kitchen and watches the bus disappear between the trees. There can't be many days to go.

LINDA

It's early in the morning. The dew is still on the grass when Hattie climbs into the back seat of the blue car. Her parents are coming to school so they can meet the teacher properly. After today, the nice bus drivers will take her. Hattie has lime green jeans and her heart is beating quick-quick. She's starting school!

They drive over hills and past yellow cornfields. Soon they come to Hardemo, where the small red houses sit close together. They drive past the little white church, right next to the school. It's built of orange bricks with wide steps in front. There are lots of cars parked next to it. Flocks of children scurry in through the door.

Hattie looks at them all.

Some of the children look so big. Almost grown-up. They're as tall as ladders. Some of them run over the grass to pick apples from the apple tree. Hattie wants to too, but she'd never dare join them. She's far too little.

Once they're in the coat area, all the new children squash in front of a yellow door. No one looks happy. Over by the bathrooms Hattie sees a girl with a pink top and turned-up nose. The girl is biting her lip and staring icily at the children around her. Hattie quickly looks away.

She's changed her mind. She doesn't want to go to school any more. She'd rather rummage about in the garden for the rest of her life.

Then the teacher comes to open the door. Hattie can go in and sit at her desk. It has a sign on it. HATTIE, someone has written in big letters. She looks around. The walls look like mustard and are quite bare. The floor is shiny green. The teacher offers all the grown-ups coffee and buns. Her mother and father are laughing with the other parents away in a corner. None of the children are laughing. They sit as quiet as little ghosts.

Hattie sneaks a look at the sign on the desk beside her. LINDA, it says. She wonders who'll come and sit there…at the same moment the chair scrapes beside her. It's the angry girl with the turned-up nose!

Linda doesn't even say hello. She just sits down and stares straight ahead. She's cute. Someone all the mothers will like because of her blonde hair, thinks Hattie. She herself has brown hair and is more the sort that mothers don't like because she talks the whole time, like a magpie.

Her stomach hurts. Bullied, she thinks. Bullied right from the start. Not a single person has talked to her yet. Especially not Linda. She sits with her mouth scrunched up like a raisin, blinking her small blue eyes.

At last the teacher has finished with coffee. He rushes over to the teacher's desk and tugs his beard. "Welcome," he says. "Now you can each tell us your name. We'll begin at the far corner."

"Mathias," says one.

"Peter," says the next. Then come Patrick, Richard and Nicholas. After Nicholas is Karin and then it's

Hattie's turn. She's nervous. Imagine if she happens to say Little Idiot instead of her proper name. She takes a breath and mumbles Hattie as fast as she can. It's over in a second. Then it's Linda's turn.

But Linda says nothing. Hattie can see that she's shaking. Her little blue eyes are shiny and her bottom lip is trembling. Linda isn't cross. She's just so nervous that she can't make a sound. Everyone waits. Linda's ski-jump nose twitches this way and that. It's covered in freckles.

"Linda," Hattie whispers at last.

Linda gives a start. "Yes," she rasps. "Linda."

Then it's Alexander's turn. Linda wipes the tears from her eyes and looks at Hattie. Hattie smiles. Linda smiles back. She has a crooked front tooth, white as a sugar lump.

And before the end of the day, the teacher is forced to move Hattie and Linda apart because they can't stop talking for a second. Linda's no longer nervous; she's the most fun person Hattie has ever met. Sweet as a princess, but she chatters on like a magpie. What a good friend!

THE
HORSE

Hattie loves school. The teacher teaches them new things every day and soon the mustard walls are covered with bright pictures. As soon as it's art time Hattie takes out her crayons and draws dogs. She writes *Tacka* at the top of all her drawings.

One of the girls in the class is called Ellen. She always draws horses. She writes *Crumb* at the top, because that's the name of her horse.

Linda draws the guinea pig she has in a cage in her room at home. Finally, she writes his name: *Roy*.

Today at break time Hattie and Linda sit on the railing next to the cars and look at a photo. It's of a little fuzzy ball with eyes shining like two headlights caught in the camera flash. This is Roy. Hattie thinks Roy is the most beautiful guinea pig in the whole world.

"Do you want to play horses?" someone suddenly asks. It's Ellen. She always wants to play horses.

In the playground is a shed with sand on the floor and an untidy pile of sticks. Ellen sets out all the sticks to make jumps. Then she gallops a couple of circuits to show how it's done. She does loops and circles and, just when she's about to crash into the wall, suddenly switches direction.

"I'm the stallion," she says. "Hattie can be the mare. And now we're starting."

They run. Linda is the trainer and stands with a

stick in her hand. If Hattie and Ellen disobey, she can hit them on the rump.

Hattie trots nicely and gets plenty of praise.

Ellen neighs and kicks backwards. "Trot!" shrieks Linda, but Ellen won't obey. She races around like a tornado, kicking all the jumps to pieces with her powerful hooves. "Trot! Trot!" shouts Linda, waving the stick. "Otherwise we'll sell you to the knackers!"

All of a sudden, Ellen completely changes. She fixes her flashing stallion eyes directly on the trainer. Linda blinks in fear. Then there's a threatening snort from Ellen. She stirs up the sandy floor with her feet and kicks at the shed walls. She backs away slowly, ready to charge. Hattie stands stock-still, staring at her.

"Halt," squeaks Linda.

The stallion shakes its head and flings its mane about. Then it lets out a loud whinny and starts to gallop.

"No!" says Linda, jumping out of the way. "We're not playing any more. I'm going."

But the stallion doesn't hear and pounds after Linda at full gallop. Linda throws away the stick and runs.

"Stop it!" Hattie cries.

Then the stallion turns and gallops at Hattie instead. Hattie rushes to Linda and grabs her arm.

"Quick!" she cries. At the last second, they throw open the shed door and leap out. They close the door, and the stallion crashes into it. Hattie finds a stick to bolt the door.

"When you calm down, we'll open it," says Linda, putting her ear against the door. The stallion replies with a kick that shakes the whole shed. Linda rubs her ear.

"Then you'll have to stay there," she says. "We'll come back in a minute and see if you're any nicer."

They run back to the railing and Linda takes out the picture of Roy.

Hattie longs to go to Linda's house and meet Roy properly. And if only she had a guinea pig too, instead of Stick the warrior cat.

After a couple of minutes, the school bell rings. Linda puts away the photo and they run inside.

Hattie goes to her desk. Linda disappears to her place across the room.

They've only had a couple of weeks of school and the teacher already looks tired. Now it's geography, and the lesson is about southern Sweden. The teacher talks about his camping trip and shows pictures of long beaches. In every photo, the teacher's wife is lying like a little sausage in a bikini.

Suddenly the teacher wrinkles his nose and looks around the classroom. "Wasn't Ellen here today?" he asks.

The horse! They forgot to let it out! Hattie looks anxiously at Linda.

Linda is as nervous as she was at the first roll call. Her little blue eyes are blinking in terror and soon wet pearls roll down her cheeks.

The teacher sees what's happening.

"Linda!" he honks. "Do you know where Ellen has got to?"

Linda can't say a word. Her face is red and her pointy nose twitches as she sniffs.

In the end Hattie puts her hand in the air.

"Yes?" says the teacher.

"Well…" Hattie begins, glancing over at Linda. "She may still be in the shed. She was locked in."

The teacher raises his eyebrows. His big beard stands out straight like the prickles on a hedgehog. "Locked in?"

Hattie nods.

"We were playing horses," she whispers.

The teacher snorts and heads for the classroom door. "No one moves till I'm back!" he cries. And then he's gone.

Hattie swallows a big lump that's stuck in her throat. The whole class is in an uproar. At least the boys are. They think Hattie and Linda have done something really clever.

The teacher comes back with the horse. By now it's no longer wild and angry. It's just sad, with red-rimmed eyes and steamed-up glasses. Hattie feels her heart sting. When the horse trots past she grabs hold of a hoof. "Sorry," she says, but it pulls away and goes to its desk.

The teacher stands at his desk. Now Hattie and Linda really get in trouble. "Imagine if the shed had caught on fire!" he says. "Or if you'd forgotten her for the whole night! What if Ellen was someone with a great fear of being shut in sheds? You need to think, think, and think again." The teacher even wants them to think what might have happened if Ellen was a person with diabetes. He wants the whole class to think about that, just because his own child at home has diabetes.

Hattie feels as if her life has ended. Now she might just as well move out to the henhouse and perch on a stick till she dies.

LOST

When Hattie arrives home that day things get even worse. Because the teacher has called to tell her mother about the horse. Her mother's face is pale.

She'd been in the living room trying out new fabric on a chair for Hattie when the telephone rang. Hattie had chosen the fabric herself, one with bananas on it. But now her mother doesn't want to finish the chair. She wants to throw the whole thing away. "How could you lock someone in like that?" she asks. Hattie has never seen her so sad.

Her mother leaves the room without saying any more. The chair with bananas on the cushions is half-finished on the floor. It all looks ridiculous.

Hattie runs out into the cold afternoon. She has her jacket and boots on and a hat with tassels.

The sun is dropping towards the horizon. Hattie steps between fir trees and disappears into the forest.

Fallen branches crunch under her feet. Hattie walks quickly. The tassels on her hat swing from side to side and her tears drip onto the moss.

Her mother doesn't want to see her again, she knows that. Nor does her father. She'll never again see Tacka or Havana, never see Stick or Linda. She decides to go far, far away so they won't have to see her. The leaves are slippery and yellow under her boots.

When she's walked a long way into the forest, she sits with her back against a tree. Tears have made her cheeks stripy. Darkness comes creeping…

And suddenly she's completely terrified!

Hattie had no idea it could get as dark as this. It's like wearing a blindfold. Her body is stiff with terror. Up in the sky small cold stars shine, but on the ground it's as dark as the underworld.

Now there are noises. Hissing and scurrying sounds nearby. It could be wolves!

"MAMAAA!" Hattie leaps to her feet; she's going to run home again. She trips over moss and branches, and yells until her voice becomes thin and hoarse. She runs a hundred miles, maybe a thousand! She's lost. The branches grab at her clothes, her boots rub and trip her up. Then she stops.

In a little clearing is a house with a light shining. It's red and run-down and all by itself. With her heart bolting, Hattie looks around. She'd rather go to her own home but she knows she'll never find the way.

She climbs the little stone steps and knocks at the door. It doesn't open. Her heart beats harder. No one comes. It's still silent inside the house.

Then she sits down and waits. She'd rather sit here the whole night than run back into the forest. A cat comes and rubs itself against her legs. They sit and look at each other for a long time. Then someone opens the door behind her back. In a tiny gap, a wrinkled man appears.

"May I come in?" says Hattie, standing up. "I have to make a phone call."

At first the man says no. He'd rather she went somewhere else to do her phoning because he doesn't like strangers. Not even if they're seven years old.

Then Hattie puts her face in her hands and sobs. The old man looks as if his ears will roll up and fall off. "Ssshhh!" he hisses, but Hattie can't be quiet. She cries even louder.

In the end the old man relents, and Hattie is allowed into the little yellow kitchen. A single lamp shines in the window. It has a stuffy smell of mashed turnips. The embroidered curtains are grubby and the floor is sticky underfoot.

The old man has a long, thin beard. He lives in the forest with fifty-eight cats. They're everywhere. On the floor, on the table, on the stove and in the sink. Even inside the open oven there's a red cat sitting and licking its paws. The old man gives it a pat on his way to a shelf with a telephone.

"Do you know the number?" he squeaks.

"Yes," says Hattie, and she takes the heavy black telephone. Soon she'll hear her mother's voice.

But no one answers at the other end. It rings on and on: ten, eleven, twelve. No one even says hello.

They don't want to answer! They're so angry they never want to talk to Hattie again, she knows it! She drops the receiver to the floor and the cats hiss and run away. Now she'll never go home again. She sobs so hard the old man is desperate.

"Shh, shh," he grumbles, wrinkling his eyebrows. "Not so loud. What's your name?"

"Hattie," Hattie sniffles.

The old man chews his tongue. "Where do you live?" he asks.

"Ängatorp," she answers.

Then the old man goes and lifts down a large kerosene lamp from a hook in a cupboard. He pulls on his boots and hat, then he puts his crusty little fist over Hattie's hand. "It's not far," he says, and swings open the door to the dark. The red cat stays in the oven.

Tall hedges line the path. The old man's light swings back and forth. Hattie sees the birch trees dancing in the yellow light and withered nettles bend underfoot. The old man strides on. Hattie gets out of breath keeping up. He squeezes her hand.

"Soon you'll be home," he says.

And at last they reach the gravel road to home. Hattie knows exactly where she is even though it's pitch-black. She can see the kitchen window at

Ängatorp shining like a warm square eye and someone's coming with a light to meet them.

"Papa!" she cries and starts running.

But it isn't Papa. It's Alf, from next door. He and her mother and father have been out searching for Hattie. That's why no one answered the telephone!

Alf says that her father has run down to the stream to look for her. And her mother has been crying. She wants to call the police and ask for a helicopter.

Hattie rushes inside and gets a lot of hugs. Her mother is shaky and says she's changed her mind about the armchair. She doesn't want to throw it away. She wants to finish it so Hattie can sit in it and be comfortable forever.

Papa comes back from the stream. He has tears in his eyes, and he keeps ruffling Hattie's hair until she gets dizzy. "Little shrimp," he says in a voice even squeakier than the old man's.

Then he takes out the map to see where Hattie has been. He looks at it and scratches his head. The old man and her mother look as well.

Then their faces turn pale and they're silent because they can see that Hattie has crossed the bog. The bog, which is deadly dangerous. You can disappear into the bog, like a little pea down the kitchen sink, and drown in a few seconds.

Then her father starts shaking. He has to hug Hattie hard, and her mother has to have a cigarette even though she doesn't smoke. "Never run away like that again," she pleads, looking at Hattie with big, frightened eyes.

Hattie promises.

She stands in the window and waves goodbye to the little old man. His lamp seesaws away in the dark, and soon she can no longer see it. Mama and Papa come and stand beside her. They're so happy she's home. Hattie is too.

SNOOPY COMES TO STAY

It's already September. Mama has put the outdoor furniture away in the barn.

Grandma and Grandpa are coming to visit, and Papa wants to cook something special to surprise them. "How about dumpling cakes?" he asks Hattie.

Hattie can hardly believe her ears. Cakes for dinner! And Papa almost never wants cake. When Hattie and her mother have afternoon tea he usually runs off to the woodshed to avoid it.

"Good idea, Papa." She applauds him.

Papa gets ready to make the batter.

"I'll probably eat quite a few of them," Hattie warns.

"Are you sure?" asks Papa.

"Yes!" Hattie promises. Who doesn't like cakes?

Caramel cakes, jam cakes, chocolate cake—she likes every kind.

Papa hums and goes on with the cake. Tacka comes and sits nearby to watch.

"Go and lie down," says Papa sternly. Tacka slinks forlornly away but she comes back almost immediately with her tongue hanging out like a dishcloth.

Soon there's a toot from the road. Grandpa and Grandma are here. Grandpa has a gray beard and a belly like a blown-up beach ball. If Hattie pounds his belly it goes boinga-boinga-boing and Grandpa laughs. He says it doesn't hurt, it feels more like a mosquito tapping with its front legs.

Grandma has small gold glasses that sit on the end of her nose. She'd probably break if Hattie pounded her belly. She's as thin as a matchstick.

They come along the hallway with happy faces. Tacka jumps and yaps, and soon Hattie comes in, hopping and yapping too. She loves it when her grandparents visit. She thrusts out the presents she's had behind her back. Grandpa gets a drawing of a house with a happy mouth and eyes. *Hello Grandpa*, it says. Grandma gets a pencil, a green one.

Then Grandpa winks at her. "Would you like a present too?" he says.

He opens his case…and out comes Snoopy! He's a white stuffed dog with long black ears and a button for a nose. On his head is a cowboy hat and his tail sticks out through a hole in his trousers. They are made of leather.

Hattie is so happy she squeals. Grandpa laughs and Grandma puts her hands over her ears.

Soon it's time for cake. Hattie flies onto her chair and picks up her knife and fork. Grandpa smacks his lips and on the floor Tacka is whimpering.

"Go and lie down!" says Papa, but Tacka takes no notice. She stays where she is, drooling. Papa growls at her a few times, but in the end he gives up. He serves cakes to everyone.

Hattie looks at hers. It's strange, not at all like a crispy little dumpling cake. More like a puffy, white jelly ball. She cuts a small piece and tastes it. Horrible. From the first mouthful, Hattie feels sick.

All the others are busy eating and enjoying them.

"Very good," says Grandpa.

"Wait till you get to the filling," says Papa. "Pork."

Pork? Hattie can hardly believe it. There should be jam or chocolate cream in cakes! Not little bits of pork with the fat still on!

"I don't like it," she says.

Papa looks baffled. "But I made extra," he says. "Eat up one at least."

"That's right," says Grandpa. "You should eat one before you leave the table."

Hattie screws up her top lip. The cake is as big as a tennis ball. She'll never manage to get it inside her. On the chair beside her Snoopy is waiting.

Suddenly something scrabbles on the floor below Hattie. It's Tacka, round eyes blinking, whiskers quivering in anticipation of fatty pork. Hattie is quick. In a flash, she grabs the cake and shoves it into Tacka's drooling mouth.

"No!" says Papa. "I saw what you did!"

But Hattie leaps from her chair and grabs Snoopy by the tail. She races up the stairs and locks the door to her room. Then she hugs Snoopy so hard his seams creak. He just smiles. He's very glad he's come to live with Hattie.

RICHARD THROWS UP

Now the frost is white on the hills when Hattie swishes past in the school bus. Today is Friday and for the final hour it's cozy Friday.

On cozy Friday everybody brings a drink and something for afternoon tea. Hattie has strawberry cordial and some of her mother's Finnish fingers. They're skinny, dry biscuits with pearl sugar on top.

Anyone who wants to can perform in front of the blackboard. Linda and Hattie have been working on a dance routine put to a song. Hattie does such high disco jumps she splits her trousers. They get lots of applause.

"Bravo," says the teacher. Then he looks at the clock. He has a slight headache because the class is so wild on Fridays, wishing for the weekend.

One boy in the class is called Richard. He's tall and thin with brown eyes and brown hair. His parents are farmers and they have at least a hundred pigs in a sty. The biggest pig is called Agnes.

Today Hattie and Richard have been squabbling since early morning. They've pulled each other's hair, chased, shoved, pinched and taunted each other. Hattie has drawn a pig on the blackboard, then written RICHARD with an arrow. Then Richard ran to the blackboard and drew a witch with warts on her face, then he wrote HATTIE.

Now that Friday is almost finished and everyone's ready to go home, Hattie wants to play one last trick. A teeny, tiny…

She goes out of the classroom. Over by the sink outside the bathroom, Richard is talking to some others in the class. He's put his drink bottle down on the box with the paper towels.

Hattie creeps up quietly. Richard doesn't notice; he has his back to her.

Then quick as a wink, Hattie snatches the drink bottle and squirts soap from the soap pump into it. Then she puts the bottle back.

Linda is nearby and has seen everything. She and Hattie stand by the big window and wait.

Soon the teacher calls that it's time to come and pack up for the day. Richard takes his drink bottle. He puts it to his mouth and tips it up. He takes a couple of mouthfuls...

And then he makes a gurgling shout! He spits drink out like an angry volcano and throws himself at the tap to rinse his mouth.

"HA HA!" Hattie squeals, and she makes a thumbs-up.

"Good work, Hattie!" Linda pats her on the back.

Richard lifts his head up and glares. As Hattie goes past he tries to punch her arm, but she's quick and ducks out of the way.

Then it's Friday evening and Hattie is at home on the sofa in the living room. She has chips and fizzy drink and is watching soap operas on TV. Her parents roll their eyes and say that the shows are rubbish, but they never miss a single episode.

In the middle of the program the telephone rings. Hattie's mother goes down to the kitchen to answer it.

After a moment she returns. "Hattie, what did you put in Richard's drink?" she asks.

Hattie's head turns cold. Richard has told on her!

"I have to know," her mother goes on, "because I'll need to call the school cleaner and ask if it was poisonous or something that could burn holes in the stomach." Her voice is soft and nice but a little worried.

Hattie sits with chip crumbs on her lap, trembling.

"It was Richard's mother who rang," says Mama. "Richard is vomiting."

Immediately Hattie feels sick. Richard wasn't supposed to get holes in his stomach or be poisoned. It was just a little joke.

"It was soap," she squeaks, and the tears come. If Richard dies from deadly poison lots of people will be angry with her. Especially Richard's parents. Everyone will think Hattie is a stupid, stupid child. Maybe she won't be able to get a job either, when she grows up.

Hattie's mother calls Ulla, the cleaner. She thinks that soap *might* have something in it that can burn holes in the stomach. But she's not sure.

Hattie has to go and lie on her bed. She feels as if she's been poisoned too, as if she might vomit. She stares straight at the wall with eyes full of tears. On the wallpaper naked angels fly around blowing trumpets. Snoopy sits in the cane chair, shaking his head.

The phone rings again. Mama runs to answer it, and then comes in to see Hattie. It was Richard's mother again. Now Richard's whole family is being sick! His mother, father and even his little sister.

Hattie wants to die! She wants to fly up to heaven and blow a trumpet! By putting soap in Richard's drink, she's poisoned the whole family. And the poor pig Agnes, is she being sick too?

"So it was a tummy bug," says her mother. "Not poisoning."

Hattie stops crying for a second. She has to breathe through her mouth because her nose is blocked with snot.

"Tubby bug…?"

Her mother nods and kisses her hot cheeks. Richard's family have gone and got a stomach bug. Hattie hasn't poisoned a single person. She feels bubbles of happiness behind her ribs. But the tears won't stop coming. Hattie puts her snotty face into her mother's soft stomach and sobs and hiccups. Mama's top gets completely wet.

"There, there," she says, stroking Hattie's head. "You don't need to cry any more."

But Hattie cries for at least half an hour. Even though she's happy, she can't stop.

The angels on the wall aren't the least bit sad. They turn wild somersaults and flap their wings. Then they play a fanfare because Richard has a tummy bug!

UGLY HAIRCUT

Back at school after the weekend, Richard looks pale. He glares at Hattie across the classroom. At break she has to be quick as a weasel so he can't catch hold of her. By the last hour she's so tired her legs are shaking.

"And don't forget!" says the teacher, as they put away their books. "It's school photos tomorrow! Dress nicely!"

When Hattie comes home and reminds her mother about the school photos, Mama goes crazy. "I'd forgotten!" she cries. "Your hair's far too long!"

She gets her kitchen scissors and asks Hattie to come. But Hattie doesn't want to because she thinks her hair is the exact right length.

"Pleeeease." Her mother pats a chair invitingly.

"Uh-uh," says Hattie. Her mother cut her hair once before and no one was particularly pleased about it. Especially not her mother.

Mama runs to her wallet and takes out some money. "What if I give you this?" She waves the money.

Hattie swipes the money and sits on the kitchen chair. For that much money Mama could practically shave her head.

But her mother isn't pleased this time either. She looks at Hattie's hair, turning her head from side to side. Whichever way she looks, she sees that it's crooked. She bites her thumbnail. "I'll call Ben," she says, running to the telephone.

Hattie can't believe it! Ben is her mother's own hair stylist in town and he's really good!

Her mother has such a nice haircut. The best part is the fringe. It points in every direction, like a tussock in the middle of her forehead. It's very modern.

They drive into town. Hattie sits in the back seat and waves at some old cows. They wave back with their tails. "Mooo!" they bellow. "See you, Hattie! Good luck with Ben."

Ben greets them in the salon. There are pictures

of women with exotic hairdos all over the walls. Short hair, long hair, in-between hair—just say what you want and Ben can do it.

Ben has a shiny shirt and two pairs of glasses sitting in a row on his narrow nose. Hattie hops up in the hairdressing chair and gets the plastic tent put on. It's like a tarpaulin, to protect her top from getting hair in it. Mama looks proud.

"What would you like?" Ben asks, peering through his glasses. "Tuft is cool."

Hattie settles into the chair. Tufts. That's what her mother has, she's sure of it. Grass tufts that stick out in all directions. She glances at Mama, who nods encouragingly.

"Yes," says Hattie. "Tufts, please."

Ben takes the scissors and starts gossiping with her mother. They have lots of friends in common to talk about. Hattie enjoys being part of it.

Snip, snip, go Ben's scissors. Hattie looks at herself in the mirror.

But he's cutting her hair strangely! It looks nothing like her mother's fringe. It's starting to look more like a shaggy lawn.

Tussocks! thinks Hattie. She wanted tussocks like Mama's. This looks horrible!

Her mother looks happy. But inside Hattie tears are starting to bubble up. She tries to hold them in so she won't hurt Ben's feelings, but the more she realizes that she looks like a stupid tennis player, the harder it is.

In the end she can't hold it in any longer. Her mouth flies open and tears rush out.

Ben almost faints. "What? What is it?" he cries, because he thinks he's cut her.

"It's ugugug-ly!" sobs Hattie.

Ben stares at her.

Her mother doesn't understand. "You wanted tuft," she squeaks.

Hattie explains that she got it all wrong. That she thought she wanted tuft because she thought that was what her mother had.

With sorrow in his voice Ben explains that her mother's fringe isn't called tuft, it's called textured spike. But now it's too late. Hattie can't go to school and be photographed with this donkey fur on her head.

Ben tries to fix it by spraying the front so it stands up like a mountain peak. "Isn't that better?" he twitters.

Hattie doesn't answer. She just wants to get out of the salon.

Her mother pays at the counter. Now she's had to pay twice, for two ugly haircuts.

But then they run into the department store and buy a hairband for Hattie. And in school no one laughs at her because Hattie is clever and pretends that she's happy to have tuft. Tuft is the latest thing. Only for the modern.

She wears her hairband for the school photos. In the group photo she wants to stand with her arms crossed. The photographer calls out that she must put her arms down and let them hang at her sides like all the others. Hattie doesn't want to look like a monkey with dangling arms. She puts them down for a moment or two, to keep the photographer happy, but when he looks in his camera, she's quick to fold them again.

And when the picture comes, she's the coolest of all. With crossed arms and a supercool tuft cut.

CANNON SHOES

Hattie pins the school photo up on the wall with the trumpet-blowing angels. Linda is in the first row because she's so small. The freckled nose points up as always.

Now Hattie quickly jumps into her clothes. The school bus will be here in ten minutes, and today's going to be fun. After school, Hattie's going home with Linda.

The whole class sings: "School is finished for todaaay! Thank you and goodbyyye!" Then they run out to the coat room and put on their outside clothes. Hattie has waterproof pants and thick gloves. Linda pulls on a second coat and lined boots. They have quite a way to walk and November is cold.

Linda lives too close to Hardemo to be picked up by the bus.

Every morning she has to start walking early through the forest to be in time for the first class. Hattie wishes she could walk to school. Linda would rather go on the bus. She sighs as they pass all the small red houses. "There's still ages to go," she says.

But there isn't really. Soon they crunch onto the gravel in Linda's back yard. Her house is also red.

"Momma!" calls Linda as they go inside. Linda's mother comes out from the kitchen. She's slim and wears a blue knitted cardigan. She sits all day sewing suspenders for a factory in town. Linda can take as many pairs of suspenders as she likes and Hattie is given a pair straight away.

In the living room hang sad paintings of sorrowful children. Tears run down their fat cheeks.

Hattie thinks these pictures are extraordinarily beautiful. At home they have only a few old paintings of stuffy old kings. All the kings have curled moustaches and shiny buttons. Papa has also done a painting, of a king called Oscar. It hangs in the hall and looks like all the others. But one thing is different. Papa has made Oscar a black man!

"I'm going to town to the shoe shop," says Linda's mother. Linda and Hattie leap about in excitement and want to go too. They're allowed!

But first there's time for Hattie to see someone she's been longing to meet. Linda shows her the way to her room. And there on the floor in a shiny cage is the guinea pig, Roy. Now Hattie can see that Roy is a fuzzy ball, not only in the photo but also in reality. He sits in a pile of hay, trembling. When Hattie puts out her hand Roy is so scared that he runs and starts biting the edge of the cage.

"You can give him a piece of cucumber," says Linda, fishing a green stump out of the hay. Hattie waves and tempts Roy with the stump, but he won't come any closer. He blinks his small black eyes and his nose twitches in fear. Just like Linda's when she's nervous!

"We're off," says Linda's mother. Hattie and Linda run to get their boots. Roy is glad to see them go.

The shop is called Cannon Shoes. On a sign above the door is a picture of a boot flying out of a cannon with sparks and smoke. "It's because they've blasted their prices to bits and sell the shoes cheap," explains Linda's mother.

Then they're inside a big room filled from top to bottom with elegant shoes. The air smells of new rubber. They go up a steep staircase with a long railing. Behind the counter, among inner soles and stray shoes, are two women wearing tight jeans and lots of makeup. They look bored.

In less than a minute, Hattie and Linda have finished looking at all the shoes. Linda's mother hasn't. She wants to stay much, much longer.

Hattie and Linda sigh. They'd forgotten how boring it is at a shoe shop. They go for another walk downstairs, through the rows of shelves.

Suddenly they stop and look at a big red booth with an opening in one side. In front of the opening is a curtain. Hattie puts her head in.

"A movie!" she cries.

Imagine, they've found a mini cinema! It shows cartoons if you put in money. They race upstairs to Linda's mother, who's trying on a shiny pair of high heels. She gives them the money and they race away again.

"Wait!" says Hattie when they're halfway down the steep staircase with the railing. "Go and stand at the bottom," she tells Linda. Hattie climbs up again with the coin in her hand. She's noticed that the railing is hollow—like a long pipe. "Caatch!" she shrieks, and she puts the coin into it. The coin rattles for a few seconds inside the pipe, then falls into Linda's hands.

"Got it!" she calls.

They send the coin several times through the pipe. It's so much fun they almost forget the movie.

But only almost. When the coin has become dizzy from all its travel, it's time. They run over to the mini cinema and put the coin into the slot.

The movie is short. It's about a rooster and a wolf who run after each other. It's over in a second. Hattie and Linda want to see more. They go and find Linda's mother, who's trying on running shoes.

Linda's mother doesn't think she's a bank and she doesn't want to give them more coins. They'll just have to have fun some other way, she says.

But Hattie can't have fun! Not without the money. She has to see the movie one more time! She thinks a minute, then she whispers to Linda: "It'll work with a price tag too. The machine won't notice what we put in it."

They grab a big price tag hanging from a boot and run back. They carefully pull the curtain so no one will see what they're up to.

The price tag is too thick for the slot. They push it in as best they can but the movie won't start. Hattie hammers with her fist on the screen. Nothing happens.

Then Linda thinks they should pull the price tag out again so that no one will notice anything. They fiddle, pull and pinch it with their nails. They even try to bite the tag out with their teeth, but it won't come. The coin box is blocked. The machine is destroyed!

Linda looks at Hattie. Her face is starting to look more and more like Roy's. Her nose quivers and her eyes are shiny.

Suddenly someone pulls back the curtain and stares at them. It's one of the counter ladies. She has a crooked ponytail that sticks out from her head like a wimple. The corners of her lipsticked mouth point to the floor. "What are you doing?" she asks.

"If you don't want to see the movie you must come out so other people can have a turn."

She sees the coin box. "What have you done? Have you broken the cinema?" She reaches in a hand with its long red nails and pulls at the price tag. It sticks like glue. "What have you put in there?"

Linda can't say a word. She just shivers. But Hattie is quick to find words. "It's a price tag from a boot," she says. "But it wasn't us. Some little kids were here before we came, and they've gone now."

The woman looks at her suspiciously. "Is that right?" she says, sucking in her cheeks. She sweeps the curtain closed and leaves. Then she stands muttering to the other woman at the counter. Both stare hard at the cinema.

Hattie and Linda run back up to Linda's mother. Now they want to go home!

But Linda's mother isn't ready yet. "Find something to play with," she says.

They sigh and look at one another. What should they do?

Then Hattie remembers the railing. They can send something else down it!

"Sure," says Linda. "What shall we use?"

Hattie thinks. Not a price tag anyway. But maybe a shoehorn? Hattie saw lots of them back at the counter.

They go over and grab a shoehorn. Hattie hopes there aren't any old bits of toe on it.

"Stop!" cries the shop lady with the ponytail. "What are you doing with that?"

Hattie's quick. "Taking it to Linda's mother. She's trying on shoes."

Then they run to the steps. Linda stays at the bottom.

"Here it comes!" Hattie feeds in the shoehorn. It goes a little way… It doesn't rattle much at all… It's stuck!

She thumps the railing but the shoehorn is stuck. Like Santa in a skinny chimney. Linda looks terrified at Hattie. Now they're in trouble. They'll be told off; they might even have to pay a fine! Tears well up inside Hattie.

But at last Linda's mother comes. "Shall we go now?"

Ye-es, they shall! They run. Hattie and Linda

throw themselves down the stairs and out to the car. They look behind. Are they being followed by angry women waving a big fine? No, it's just Linda's mother with her shoe bags. They cheer as they leave Cannon Shoes behind them. Oh, how wonderful to be away from there!

ADVENT

Hattie has hugged Snoopy so often with grubby hands that one day her mother puts him in the washing machine. When he comes out, all the stuffing in his neck has gone down to his belly, and his head hangs like a wilted melon. Hattie is angry. Now Snoopy will be bent over for the rest of his life just because her mother wanted to put him in the washing machine. Her mother says she can open Snoopy up and put a stick in his neck.

But Hattie doesn't want that. She thinks he'd rather stay floppy. She takes Snoopy outside. They sit on the swing and grieve over what's happened.

"Look, Snoopy." Hattie holds his head up so he can see. "It's snowing."

Winter has arrived.

But it will be a long wait before Hattie can pull the sled from the barn. These snowflakes are so small and fragile, they melt before they land. She longs so badly for snowmen, angels and candles that it makes her dizzy. But even more than that, she longs for Advent.

And then it finally arrives, with lots of Advent calendars on the walls in the house. On other mornings when Hattie has to get out of bed, she takes forever. Her eyes won't open, and her legs feel as if they're stuck with cement to her mattress.

But not now. She shoots up like a rocket and runs down the stairs. She opens the most boring calendar first, the one from the Swedish church. Jesus looks out from every window. He has a beard and is painted in blurry soft tints.

Then she opens the one from the ICA shop, with happy people enjoying themselves at the supermarket. Hattie is happy too at the supermarket. She wants to work at the checkout at ICA when she grows up.

Second to last, she opens the chocolate calendar, and that leaves only the best one—the calendar her mother made as a present. It's as big as a window and has a green fir tree on it. Small packets tied with red string hang from all the branches.

Her mother has been sitting at her desk for several days fixing and wrapping. Hattie hasn't been allowed to go in for a sneak peep, even for a second! But when her mother went to make dinner, Hattie crept in and had a look anyway. It doesn't matter. She's just as happy when she opens them.

She finds a perfumed eraser and a plastic monster. Everything is lovely. And her mother has decorated the house with Advent stars.

The school cafeteria is also decorated. Beautiful angels, ugly elves and gaudy prayers embroidered by the women at Red Cross.

Henrika is one of the lunch cooks. She's crazy. Even when the children say "a tiny, tiny bit" she still gives them a huge spoonful, enough for a hungry sailor. And you have to eat cabbage salad and you're not allowed to throw it away. Henrika stands guarding the bins like a mad panther.

One day there's blood pudding for lunch. Linda's

nose quivers all the way to the cafeteria. She can't eat blood pudding. It's as if a door closes in her throat when she has to swallow.

"Say that you have a stomachache," says Hattie when they've hung up their coats. The Advent candles shine in the window. "Then you only get one slice."

Linda blinks with her little blue eyes and nods.

They wait their turn for lunch.

"I only need one because I have a stomachache," Linda whispers when she gets to Henrika.

Henrika gives her two slices. "If you have a stomachache you need to eat," she says. "Otherwise it won't go away. Relish?"

Linda swallows. "Yes," comes from her mouth so quietly it almost can't be heard.

Linda sits shaking with Hattie beside her. The long table is full of children forcing down the pudding. But no one has as much trouble eating it as Linda. "It sticks in my throat," she says, wrinkling her nose. "I can't."

Hattie also hates blood pudding. She puts small pieces in her mouth and takes big gulps of milk.

Soon the room is empty. Only Henrika is left. And, at one of the long tables, Linda and Hattie. Hattie's plate is empty. Linda's is full, so she'll sit there till break is over.

Quickly Hattie pinches one of Linda's black slices and puts it on her own plate. Linda looks happy.

But Henrika calls from the kitchen: "I saw that! You have to eat up your own food by yourself."

She comes over at speed and looks sternly at Hattie. "Put the blood pudding back!" she says. "With your fork! And then you can leave because you've finished!"

Hattie looks at the table. She slowly pushes the slice of pudding over to Linda's plate with her fork. "I'll be waiting by the coats," she whispers, and disappears.

Hattie waits half an hour before Linda appears. She looks pale.

"I ate it," she says. "Henrika sat beside me and watched." Linda has to sit on the bench to rest. Her hands are shaking as she wipes the tears from her cheeks.

It's so unfair, Hattie thinks. No one would ever

force the cook to eat blood pudding till she was almost sick. "Henrika should be punished," she says.

Linda tightens her lips and nods earnestly.

They sit for a long time and wonder what they can come up with.

The triangular lights glimmer in the window. Linda sits up. "Did you know that you can get a shock if you put water on electrical things?" she asks.

Hattie does. And all at once they have a plan!

They can hear rattling in the kitchen. Henrika is busy washing dishes. Hattie and Linda pull out the wall plug to one of the Advent lights. Then they unscrew one of the small light bulbs and fetch water from the bathroom. They splash a little into the hole, then put back the lightbulb, loosely so that Henrika will have to screw it in herself.

Then they run away. In the morning when Henrika comes along and plugs in the lights and screws in the lightbulb, she'll get a shock. Ha ha! Serves her right! It might teach her to cook better food too.

When school is over Linda walks home and Hattie takes the bus.

After a few hours it's nighttime. It's amazing how much thinking you do in the night. Hattie lies in bed, ready to go to sleep. Then she realizes that it might be quite dangerous mixing water and electricity. Even quite deadly dangerous!

Have they murdered Henrika? Hattie imagines her lying like a little charred skeleton in the playground, with a crooked finger pointing straight at Hattie.

"Her. She's the one who murdered the cook!"

It's a dreadful night. She dreams about Henrika's poor family and grandchildren, who are crying in sorrow. A dreadful night. And a dreadful morning. A dreadful, dreadful journey on the bus.

Linda meets Hattie by the fence when she gets off. Her blonde slept-on hair is all over the place. Of course, she's also had a terrible night.

They run to the cafeteria and look in through the window. Is Henrika lying there gripping a light bulb and smoking? No, the floor is empty. The Advent lights aren't shining. They bang on the door, shouting and calling. After an eternity Henrika comes out from the kitchen to open it.

"What is it?" she growls.

"We think we might have left our hats here yesterday," says Hattie.

"Hmm," mutters Henrika, letting them in. Then she goes back to the kitchen.

They rush in. Hattie unscrews the lightbulb and puts her finger in.

"Was it wet?" asks Linda.

Not especially. A little damp, perhaps. But they must stop Henrika from plugging it in. They can't let on that they were trying to electrocute her on purpose.

After a while Henrika in the kitchen hears an almighty noise.

"Oh, oh!" shrieks Linda.

"Oh, oh dear!" cries Hattie.

Henrika comes rushing, angry, with flour in her puffy hairdo. Why are they oh-oh-ing? she wants to know.

"Well…" Hattie explains: it happens that they got so hot and sweaty from looking everywhere for their hats that Hattie had to go and get a cup of water.

"That's right," says Linda.

"Yes," continues Hattie. Then she was just going to sit in the window for a little rest, but she tripped over and spilled water—right onto the Advent lights.

She points at the lightbulb. Henrika stares.

"So, you should probably be careful when you plug them in," says Hattie. "Be careful that you don't get a shock."

"Yes," says Linda.

Henrika doesn't understand a thing. "Is that right?" is all she says, raising an eyebrow.

But Hattie and Linda run away, their hearts free again. It's so great that Henrika is alive!

THE
LAST DAY BEFORE CHRISTMAS BREAK

One evening the whole family is in the kitchen doing Christmas baking.

"Shall we make a gingerbread house?" asks Papa.

Hattie agrees straight away and the gingerbread dough comes out of the fridge. It's been resting in there for several days.

They knead and they roll. Hattie has planned a multi-level house with balconies and little gingerbread people in the windows. Papa thinks it would be just as much fun to do something a little less complicated. The duck house in the yard, for example. After they've squabbled a bit, they decide on a compromise. They'll make the duck house but with small gingerbread pigs on the roof. Soon they're under way, cutting out brown walls.

It's lovely in the little kitchen. It's dark outside the window, and no cars pass by. After a couple of hours, they can stick the pieces together with burnt sugar. And when the pigs are baked, Hattie sticks them on the peaked roof. The house is perfect. They put it on the table in the big room and in a second Tacka the dog comes in to sniff. Then she sits at the table all evening and whines and pants, but she's not given even a crumb.

Hattie's mother doesn't like making gingerbread houses. She bakes Norwegian cakes instead, much taller than the little duck house. They're almost as tall as Hattie!

The cakes sway like fragile card houses on the floor and her mother runs around putting on the icing. Hattie's grandmother is from Norway, which is why Hattie's mother enjoys making Norwegian cakes.

Although they're so tall, Mama's cakes never collapse and break. Whereas Hattie's buns slump, even though they're only small snails called saffron buns. But it doesn't matter. Mama thinks a collapsed snail tastes just as good as one from a master chef.

It's not long before the teacher says one afternoon in school: "Don't forget to bring afternoon tea tomorrow, for our party. Goodbye."

"Goodbye!" shouts the class, running out. They're all so happy that the holidays are near. Hattie struggles into her layers and Linda puts her arms into the two coats. Their hair is electric and stands out from their heads like tall grass on a prairie.

"What will you bring for afternoon tea?" asks Hattie. "Have you made gingerbread?"

Linda shakes her head. "No-oo." She shrugs. "We haven't had time." Then she laughs. "Momma just sews and sews."

Their noses go red when they're out in the cold. At last there's snow on the ground. It crunches under their boots and glistens on the fields.

Soon Hattie is sitting on the bus. Through the window she watches Linda's little blue coat disappearing through the fir trees. And that gives her an idea!

When the school bus collects Hattie the next day she has one of her saffron snails and two gingerbread hearts in an old glass box in her backpack. In her hand she carries a supermarket bag. All the way to school she sits completely still with the bag on her lap.

In the classroom it's pretty and festive. In the final art class, all the children cut out snowy stars from white paper, and now the stars are taped on the high window. *Happy Holidays*, the teacher has written on the blackboard, and red ribbons hang from the ceiling.

Now they're all sitting at their desks. The teacher lights the four candles in the candleholder on his desk. Then he turns off the lights.

"Welcome to the last school day before Christmas," he says quietly. Then he takes out small plastic mugs and four thermoses. "Everyone can come up for glogg."

Soon there's a jostling crowd at the desk. The glogg might run out and there won't be enough for the last person! Hattie hurries over.

At last she has a plastic mug in her hand. It's hot and she has to hurry back to her desk to put it down.

Then everyone takes out their afternoon tea. Hattie places the snail and the two hearts on her desk. All the children around her do the same:

saffron snails and gingerbread. Hattie looks over at Linda's desk. There are two dry crackers beside her little mug of glogg.

Then Hattie takes out her bag, puts in her hand and carefully pulls out what she's brought with her. It's the duck house. Hattie asked at home and Papa was happy for Linda to have it. People should have gingerbread for Christmas. She goes over to Linda's desk.

"Happy Christmas," she says, setting down the house. "You can eat it."

Linda looks at the house with her mouth open. The crooked tooth shines white in the dark. But then the sides of her mouth go up and Linda's eyes sparkle, blue and happy.

"Thank you," she says. "Happy Christmas!"

But she won't ever eat the house, she says. She'll save it in the bookcase as a decoration!

The teacher plays Christmas carols. Everyone in the class is quiet and solemn as if they're at a funeral.

But only for a short while. Soon the gingerbread and the saffron snails are eaten up and then it's hard to keep still. Everyone feels their legs squirming for the holidays, and soon they're so bubbly and chatty that the teacher has to put a stop to it. For a difficult half hour, they sit and listen to the end of the Christmas story. Then the teacher turns the lights back on. "Happy Christmas!" he calls.

"Happy Chrisss-stmas!" everyone shrieks, and they all rush out. The sticky glogg mugs stay behind on the desks.

"What have you wished, for a Christmas present?" Hattie asks by the coats.

"The pony castle," says Linda, pulling the supermarket bag over the gingerbread house.

"Me too!" says Hattie. "Do you think you'll get it?"

Linda shrugs. "Nah," she says and laughs as usual. "But it doesn't matter."

"I don't think I'll get it either," says Hattie. Then she laughs too, even though she thinks life will end without the castle. But she doesn't want to tell Linda that.

They say goodbye to each other. Soon Hattie is on the bus watching Linda disappear through the fir trees. The bag is dangling from her hand. Hattie's heart bolts inside her. Now it's the holidays!

CHRISTMAS

At last it's the twenty-fourth of December. Hattie rushes down to the living room and takes a deep breath. The day before they decorated the tree, and now her lungs are filled with pine tree scent and the smell of a scrubbed floor. When Hattie gets that floor cleaner smell in her nostrils, she's so happy she could cry. It means Christmas.

On a white sideboard stands a little plastic crib. The baby Jesus lies in it with a blue swaddling cloth on a pile of hay. Around it are the three wise men and Joseph and Mary, who are holding their hearts. A little further away is a tired donkey with his ears back. He probably wants food.

Under the tree is a heap of presents. Hattie wants to throw herself on the floor and feel every single one.

There are square ones and round ones, soft and hard. And maybe the pony castle is in there somewhere.

Hattie and Linda aren't the only ones who want a pony's pink dream castle. The whole class wants one, except for the boys. It has three high towers with violet tops and a drawbridge you can wind up and down. Hattie knows that if she's given the pony castle this evening she'll never feel sad again about anything. But she's worried…

For a whole month she's been asking Mama about the castle. Her mother just said: "Well, we'll see about that on Christmas Eve." And a few days ago something happened that can't be explained.

They were standing at the sink making pickled herrings. And suddenly Hattie's mouth opened and out came the strangest words:

"I don't really want the castle. I won't be sad if I'm given something else."

"Hmmm," was all her mother said.

And Hattie can't understand why she said that. Because she knew all the time that it wasn't true. The pony castle is the only thing that matters in the whole world. But now as she stands and stares at the presents under the tree, it looks more and more as if it isn't there.

She goes out to the kitchen.

"Good morning," her father chirps, cutting a piece of ham for his sandwich.

"Morning," mumbles Hattie. She sits on the sofa and takes a bite of her sandwich. It's hard to chew. Every second that passes makes her more nervous. And it's such a long time until presents.

The last clip in Donald Duck's Christmas Eve selection is about Chip and Dale going to Mickey Mouse's house and getting into a fight with Pluto. Then Jiminy Cricket sings about wishing on a star. It's a lovely moment. Papa is busy with food in the kitchen and Hattie sits close to Mama on the TV sofa. Her mother smells good and she looks nice in her skirt and blouse. Snoopy also looks nice. He's wearing a little Christmas hat.

Then they hear tooting on the gravel road. That means Grandma and Grandpa have arrived. At last they can eat! In the dining room everything is ready. There's pate, sausages, cheese and herrings.

The ham is round and rosy on a plate and in a clay pot there's something terrible: pigs' trotters. They have their hooves still on them and tufty hairs clinging to the rind. Hattie stands with her nose over the pot and sniffs. Brrr! She'd never want to put her teeth into anyone's foot.

Her mother doesn't want to eat pigs' trotters either. She and Hattie look out through the window while the others eat them.

"Silly," says Papa, sucking between the toes of one hoof. He thinks that you don't know good food if you can't find room for a pig's trotter or two between herrings and ham. But Hattie and her mother take no notice. They're proud of being proper bad fooders.

Hattie eats her Christmas food quickly and wants everyone else to do the same. But that's not how it is. As always the grown-ups sit at the table for hours. She knows they drag it out on purpose. She has to run into the living room to look at all the presents. What if the castle isn't there!

After an eternity Mama goes to make coffee. Then she puts out the Christmas chocolates in the living room and everyone sits on the sofas. Now

Hattie can pass around the presents. She looks at the pile under the tree. If the castle is there somewhere, it will be a big package.

She finds a large box wrapped in Christmas paper and reads the tag aloud: "To Hattie." She quickly opens it.

Inside are ski boots. "Thanks," she says and flies on to the next one. It has *To Hattie* on it also. She's about to pull on the ribbon.

"Wait for that one," says Mama.

Papa agrees. "It's no fun if you open all the big ones first. Try a few small ones now."

Hattie dives onto the other presents. She's given a warm hat, hair ties, the *Big Book of Ghosts* and a whole salami. Salami is the best Hattie-food she knows!

She leafs through the *Big Book of Ghosts*. The pages drip with blood and you can read about all the terrible creatures in the world—vampires, witches and the headless rider. At the back are instructions on how to get in touch with the ghost world. You can call the White Lady, speak to spirits and read your own spit. Hattie feels cold shivers run

up and down her spine. But maybe she wouldn't mind meeting the White Lady…

Her mother, father, grandma and grandpa all get lots of presents. There are paintings and beaded mats and other artworks. Everyone is pleased.

Soon Hattie has opened all the presents. There's only one left, the big one that her mother and father wanted her to wait for. *To Hattie.* Her hands are shaking as she takes off the paper…

And in a shimmer of pink the pony castle appears! She explodes with happiness. Now she'll be happy till the earth stops turning!

Hattie is also given silver cutlery and embroidered cloths from Grandma and Grandpa. They don't count. She's so pleased with the pony castle that she can't be sad about a newly polished cheese cutter from 1942.

Before Hattie goes to bed she calls Linda. Her mother answers. "Is Linda there?" asks Hattie.

"Wait a minute," she says.

It is a minute before Linda's voice squeaks in Hattie's ear. "Hello?"

"It's Hattie," says Hattie. "I got the castle."

She pauses a moment. If Linda didn't get a castle it doesn't feel so good. "Did you?" she asks carefully.

Linda laughs a bit and says: "Yes. I did too."

And then Hattie laughs as well. They chat for a little while and count their presents. Linda has been given two T-shirts and a water dispenser for Roy.

Soon Hattie yawns. "See you in school," she says.

"See you," replies Linda and she puts the phone down. Hattie rushes like an arrow through the house and into the living room. There stands the castle, like pink marzipan. What a perfect Christmas Eve.

THE
WAFFLE

In no time school starts again. When the children step into the classroom a surprise is waiting for them. A new teacher! But the old teacher is still here because the new one is only staying for a month. She's training to be a teacher in town and has come to learn about real life in a school. Her hair is yellow and wavy, and her cheeks are pitted. She speaks as quietly as a mouse and almost never smiles.

She stands at the blackboard to introduce herself: "I come from Trosa," she tells the class.

Then Hattie laughs so hard that the roof almost lifts because Trosa means underpants. Soon all the others are laughing with her and the teacher frowns.

"Shh!" she hisses, glowering at Hattie. "Stop being so silly!"

After that she's cross for several days and whenever Hattie puts her hand up to ask for help the teacher says only a few words.

One Wednesday the whole class is outside the classroom putting on their outside clothes. It's morning break.

"Who wants to call the White Lady?" Hattie asks. Everyone goes stone quiet. They look at each other with scared faces. "I've been reading about it in the *Big Book of Ghosts*," says Hattie. "The White Lady is a free-floating spirit. She'll come if you know how to call her."

It's thrilling, though, and everyone wants to join in. Hattie explains how it works. You go into the bathroom and lock the door. You're not allowed to turn on the light. Then you stand in front of the mirror, looking into it, and you say, "White Lady, White Lady, come hither," three times in a row. Then you'll see a sad figure—completely white— appear in the mirror. And after that the White Lady can appear at any time, when you least expect it!

Everyone starts chattering. They're going to call on the living dead! Someone from the Other Side!

"Who wants to start?" Hattie asks. The chatter stops instantly. The girls shake their heads and the boys look at the floor. When it comes down to it, no one dares.

"I'll go then," says Hattie. "If someone comes with me."

The boys scrape their feet and their eyes wander. They mumble that they might go skating instead, down on the rink.

Hattie crosses her arms and stares at them. "Does no one dare?" she asks. "In that case it won't happen."

Then there's someone with blonde hair and a turned-up nose who steps out from the group. It's Linda and she dares.

They close the door behind them. The cowards stay behind, wide-eyed and certain this is the last they've seen of Hattie and Linda. Certain that the White Lady will kidnap them from inside the mirror!

The door has a gap at the bottom so it's not properly dark inside the bathroom. They stand side by side and look into the mirror. Linda begins in a shaky voice: "White Lady, White Lady, come hither."

Hattie continues: "White Lady, White Lady, come hither."

Linda concludes: "White Lady, White Lady... come hither?"

Now she could come at any moment. Hattie's heart beats hard. She peers into the mirror for traces of the poor pale woman.

But the only little woman she sees is herself. And Linda. They stand there with winter-pale faces, blinking. The White Lady doesn't dare either, when it comes down to it. They stare at the mirror until they're tired of it and then they leave.

"Nothing happened," says Hattie. But the whole class looks spooked anyway and soon Hattie understands why. The new teacher has found them, and she's angry. Her pitted cheeks are quivering.

Hattie gets a long, long lecture for involving the class in such dangers. The new teacher happens to know lots of children who have become sick in the head from playing White Lady.

Hattie says that she can't help what happened to those other children. In her own head she feels as fresh as a cucumber.

"That's not the point," the teacher replies, her voice reaching falsetto. "Things like this can scar the brain for life. And anyway, the White Lady doesn't exist; it's a joke. Don't do it again!"

She leaves.

Hattie's face is burning hot. She can't understand what there is to yell about if the White Lady is only a joke. The whole class looks at her as if she's fallen for a trick.

"I knew the whole time that she didn't exist," says Karin. Ellen agrees.

"Let's go skating," says Mathias.

They all run away. Only Hattie and Linda are left.

"Shall we go too?" asks Linda.

Hattie's not sure. What she really wants to do is hide under a snowdrift in the forest and never come out. Everyone suddenly got so cross. But the book said that the White Lady exists! It's just a matter of doing everything properly in the bathroom.

They head outside through the school's high wooden doors. Everything feels unfair. Their skin tingles in the cold and from down at the skating rink come the shouts of their classmates. They're just about to go down the path when it happens! Hattie freezes and stares over at the cafeteria.

"Wait!" she whispers, holding a hand out to Linda. Linda stares with wide eyes in the same direction. And then they see her. For a short second, they glimpse the White Lady. She's standing behind a downpipe and she gives them a mischievous little wave. Then she's gone.

They look at each other with their mouths wide open. Linda's face is shining, and inside Hattie it feels as if a big balloon is being blown up. They've seen her! The White Lady!

That evening it's parent–teacher meetings. Hattie goes with her mother and father. They meet the teacher and the new teacher. There are coffee and buns on the teacher's desk but Hattie's parents are too nervous for that. Not Hattie. She's already eaten three buns by the time the teacher starts talking.

He has mostly nice things to say. Hattie does her homework, can add and subtract, and puts her hand up often. Mama and Papa smile. Papa's cheeks puff with pride when the teacher says that Hattie writes the longest essays in the class. Even when the teacher says the essays are even a little too long sometimes, Papa shines like the summer sun. "Little shrimp," he mumbles and laughs.

"Hrm," says the new teacher. "What Hattie should think about is not being so cocky. She has too much to say."

Mama and Papa stop smiling.

In the car on the way home they mutter that only proper teachers should be allowed to speak up in parent–teacher talks. Then Hattie hears her father joke that the new teacher's face is like a waffle because of the holes in her cheeks. Her mother giggles.

"Yes!" cries Hattie. "A waffle!"

Her parents press their lips closed. "Shush," says Mama. "It's not funny. It's just your father being silly."

But Hattie heard what Papa said. Ha ha! She thinks the teacher looks like a waffle too.

SEVEN
YEARS OLD

When they get home from the parent–teacher meeting, Hattie's mother runs into her room and locks the door. Hattie knows what she's doing in there.

"Can I come in?" she calls through the keyhole with her syrupy-sweetest voice.

"No!" her mother replies, and Hattie hears the wonderful rustle of wrapping paper. Tomorrow she turns seven years old!

She stands for a while outside the door and whines just like Tacka does.

"I'll put tape over the keyhole if you don't go away," Mama says.

Then Hattie runs away. It's not even a month since Christmas but she's already longing for more presents!

At bedtime she lies for hours blinking at the ceiling. It's made of planks. The round knots look like thousands of flying saucers whizzing around in space. They're looking for a place to land but they never find one.

Hattie squints. The bed is hot and uncomfortable. Snoopy's awake too, thinking about her birthday. The floppy head hangs to his belly and the long ears are spread onto the pillow. Hattie lifts one. "What do you think I'll get for my present?" she whispers.

"Skis," Snoopy thinks. Because he's seen her parents smuggling in a very long package. Hattie saw it too. Snoopy's probably right.

"But what else do you think?" she mumbles and a yawn slips out. "What else could there be?"

Snoopy doesn't answer. He's fallen asleep. So Hattie pulls the soft, white body closer. She feels her eyelids become heavy. Snoopy's fur tickles under her nose. At last she falls asleep too.

"Happy birthday to you, happy birthday to you!" Her parents' voices find their way to her ears. Hattie blinks tiredly, then when she remembers what day it is, she bounces awake and sits up in bed. Snoopy's been awake for hours. Now they're in the doorway, her mother and father with all the presents. Papa is carrying a tray with a cloth and flowers. Soon Hattie sits in a pile of presents.

She is given skis exactly as Snoopy thought. They're thin and racer-quick. A pair of poles comes in the same package. The absolutely best present is the game of Ronia, the Robber's Daughter with Borka, Lovis, the rumphobs and all. Hattie loves board games! As long as she wins.

In the first class at school everyone stands up, except for Hattie. They sing, "Happy birthday to you, happy birthday to you, happy birthday, dear Hattie, happy birthday to you!" The teacher says, "Hip, hip," and the class shouts, "hooray!" Hattie sits at her desk and enjoys it.

"I'm first in the class to have my birthday," she says at morning break. Then Ellen and Karin say that it's much better to have your birthday in summer because January is so close to Christmas and you've already had a whole lot of presents.

A birthday in January is all wrong, they think. Hattie looks at the floor.

Then Linda says that it's good to have your birthday in January. And that Ellen and Karin have big bottoms. And Hattie is happy again!

When Karin and Ellen have run away, Linda puts her hand in her pocket. It bulges as if there's a whole roll of toilet paper in there. "I have something," she says, pulling out a package. She's painted the paper herself, with Roy on it, and she's written, *Happy Birthday Hattie from Linda.*

Hattie opens it carefully so the painting isn't spoiled. "Thank you!" she says, pulling out two stretchy bands with little clasps at their ends.

"It's sleeve holders," Linda explains. She shows on Hattie's shirt how to use the clasps to keep her sleeves up. "For when you do baking or dishes," she says. "Momma's making sleeve holders for the factory now. She's finished with suspenders."

Hattie wears the sleeve holders all day. They're pink.

In the evening she tests her new Ronia, the Robber's Daughter game with her parents. They all sit down in the living room and set up the board.

Soon they are deep in the dark Matt's Wood. You have to get to Bear Cave alive and as quick as you can. Every time you throw the dice, you take a card from the pile on the table. The cards are terrible. They might say something like: Wild fiends! Everyone must jump back heaps of steps or: Underground fog! Danger, danger! Throw the dice to see if you die! Sometimes they just say: Nothing much happens.

Hattie is on tenterhooks every time she has to pick a card. Behind every tree stump new dangers lurk. She really wants to go straight to Bear Cave without meeting all the terrible things along the way.

Her parents think nothing of the danger. They just shrug their shoulders as they dangle over the Gap of Hell with only a spindly leather strap around their waists. But Hattie's going to faint!

And quite suddenly she's begun to cheat. She hardly noticed it happening, except that she can't bear another second in Matt's Wood, with all the monsters waiting to eat her up. It feels so real: if she doesn't cheat, she'll die!

She takes a card from the pile. She doesn't even

look at it. "Nothing much happens," she says, quick as a wink putting the card back at the bottom of the pile. Then it's her father's turn. Then it's her mother's, then Hattie's again. "Nothing much happens." She puts the card at the bottom of the pile.

Soon Hattie has run all the way through Matt's Wood without meeting even an ant. Her parents think it's strange that they get the dangerous cards so often, and Hattie doesn't get a single one. When Hattie says for the fourteenth time, "Nothing much happens," and is about to put the card back, her mother is quick.

"Let's see it," she says and snaps the card away. Then she reads out: "Bottomless ravine. Jump right in."

Her mother and father are cross. They think it's no fun to play with a cheater. Hattie glares at the floor and feels tears looming. It's actually not as easy as they think to be a child in Matt's Wood! How can they ask someone who's only seven years old to jump down into the bottomless ravine with a heel kick and a yell?

"But those are the rules," says Mama. "It can't be

helped if it's dangerous, you have to do it anyway. Otherwise the game doesn't work."

It's so unfair. Her parents understand nothing! They should play in teams so the grown-ups can protect the children and sacrifice themselves when someone has to drop into a deadly ravine. And where is Birk when you need him? In the movie, at least there are two of them thrashing around together in the waterfall. Hattie cries and shudders, thinking of the ravine. She doesn't want to die!

Then she doesn't need to. "We'll finish playing another time," says her mother.

They pack up the board and say goodbye to Ronia, the Robber's Daughter.

She'll have to do the best she can among the gray wolves. Hattie dries the tears from her cheeks. At least she's made it out alive from the dangerous Matt's Wood!

THE LONG SKI TOUR

Ronia, the Robber's Daughter can stay in the wardrobe until someone wants to see her again. But not the new skis. Only a few days later it's time to "go on tour" at school!

The teacher explains: Going on tour means that you don't go fast and compete to see who's best, but you ski gently for a long time and enjoy the outdoors.

The teacher comes from town and always wants the children to get out and enjoy the outdoors. He forgets that they've grown up in the country and have seen nothing but the outdoors their whole lives.

He stands in front of them in the playground looking cheerful. Snow crystals glisten in his big beard and his breath steams. It's minus eighteen degrees and everyone is wearing hats like bank robbers, except in bright patterns.

Hattie's already shivering. Her clothes are so thick she can hardly bend over to clip on her skis, but still the cold reaches right to her bare skin.

"Off we go!" the teacher commands. He's going first. All the children will go in the middle, and at the back is the teacher with the pockmarked skin—Waffle. Hattie is second to last, with only Waffle behind her. They ski off over the playground.

It's hard work and boring. The new skis aren't at all racer-quick; they're as slow as any old pair of planks. Her boots are wet in two seconds flat and her toes turn to ice in three.

"Keep up!" calls the teacher. "Keep an even distance and try to avoid gaps in our convoy!"

But someone has already stopped, and the convoy looks more like a necklace with several dropped beads. "Stop, I've lost a ski!" "Wait, she's lost a ski!" they shriek over each other.

The teacher sighs. He wants a pleasant ski tour, not ten-pin bowling.

Hattie grimaces with her stiff face. Minus degrees

cling like cold leeches to your body.

"How far is it to go?" she calls to the teacher.

He laughs. "We're still in the school grounds! We'll go past the church, down to the forest and take a swing around the paddocks before we come back!" He is overjoyed at how far they still have to go.

Hattie doesn't know what to do. She wiggles her aching toes. They feel as if they could fall off at any moment, like ten small icicles.

She turns around and sees Waffle struggling right behind her. The pitted cheeks have white flecks and her lips are completely blue. Waffle meets her eyes with a desperate look. "Nothing for it but to keep going," she says.

Just across the playground is the nice warm school. Hattie turns and skis on with a heavy heart. There is still so far to go.

Then they come to a ditch that runs straight through the field, forming a deep moat. The water in the bottom is frozen and now the class has to cross over it.

The teacher goes first to show how it's done. He steps sideways down the steep edge, stabbing with his poles to keep him steady. It looks elegant. He climbs up in the same way and soon he's on the other side, waving to the next in line. "Just do exactly as I did!" he calls.

The convoy begins to step down into the ditch. Soon they're all over, except for Hattie and Waffle. The teacher urges the new teacher on with his pole. "Off I go again with these ones, and you can help the last one!" he calls. The line of small skiers moves off.

Hattie looks at Waffle.

Waffle blinks at the deep ditch.

"Oh my goodness," she mumbles and swallows. Then she drags in a deep breath.

Hattie sees that she's wearing thin finger gloves, and on her yellow hair there's only a little beret like a button.

"Okay," says Waffle, beginning to climb down in her skis. She doesn't go sideways as the teacher showed them but lets the points of her skis go first. She reaches out her hand. "Come on, I'll steady you," she says.

Hattie takes hold and shuffles carefully forwards. Waffle sways like a bendy flagpole. When Hattie leans forward, they both tumble right down into the deep ditch. Their skis come off, and Hattie finds herself headfirst in a drift. Hard lumps of snow have crept under her collar.

Waffle snorts as she scrambles to her knees. "Did you hurt yourself?" she asks with anxious eyes.

Hattie shakes her head. They can hear the teacher shouting from a distance. "Are you all right? Are you all right?" He comes swishing back as fast as his long skis can carry him.

Waffle is quick. "We're hurt!" she cries, looking at Hattie. "Did you hurt yourself?" she asks.

Hattie blinks. Waffle looks desperate. And then Hattie feels sure: "Yes! Yes!" she calls to the teacher. "I hurt my leg! I got a pole in the stomach!"

Waffle gets up slowly. "We can't go on," she says. "Someone has to take Hattie back to the classroom to see how badly hurt she is."

The teacher nods importantly. "Quite right," he says. "You two go up to the classroom and rest. We will complete the ski tour."

He swishes back to the front again and the long line toils towards the horizon.

Waffle takes their skis in her arms, then she and Hattie climb out and head for the schoolhouse.

It's much quicker to walk than to ski. In a few minutes Hattie is sitting in the classroom wearing just her long underwear and T-shirt. She has her feet on the radiator. The heat tingles in her toes.

The whole morning she sits there painting ice cream cones on big sheets of paper. Sometimes she looks at Waffle at her desk. Waffle looks back with a little smile. "How nice it is to be inside," she says.

Hattie nods. It is.

THE CHURCH CHILDREN'S HOUR

Then it's not many days before Waffle says goodbye to the class. A month has gone by. She's given a bunch of flowers and then she goes around and hugs everyone. "Goodbye, Hattie," she says when it's Hattie's turn. Then she gives her a wink and smiles. Hattie winks back. They've become friends after all.

When Waffle has gone, the teacher hands out pieces of green paper. "These are from the church, about their children's hour," he says. "Anyone who wants to can go."

Hattie folds up the paper and puts it in her bag.

At home, she shows it to her parents. Papa frowns right away. "That sort of thing is absurd," he says.

But her mother asks if Hattie wants to go.

Hattie nods, because it has actually become a little tedious not living next door to anyone. Some days she only has the sheep on the farm to talk to.

Her mother reads the note out loud. "Register with Irene. First meeting on Thursday in the church hall."

She goes to the telephone and Hattie follows. Her father pads along behind. He pokes Hattie in the back when her mother starts to dial the number.

"You'll get money if you don't go," he whispers.

Her mother hears him. "Stop it," she says with an edge to her voice and her father sulks away.

Irene says Hattie is very welcome to the Church Children's Hour. "She sounds nice." Mama smiles as she puts down the phone. Hattie can't wait.

When the time comes, Mama drives Hattie to the church hall. It's right next to school.

"See you afterwards," says her mother. Hattie goes in through the little old wooden gate.

There are bright pictures on the walls. They show people and lambs sitting and cuddling each other. They look peaceful. A lot more peaceful than Hattie feels mumbling to the sheep on the farm back home.

Irene is round and has yellow curls like a helmet on her head. She looks kindly at everyone new. Hattie waves to Ellen and Karin, who have sat down at a round table. Linda didn't want to come to the Church Children's Hour. Just like Hattie's father, she thought it sounded silly.

They sit for a long time talking with Irene. She tells stories from the life of Jesus and all the time she shines like a sun. Hattie feels her heart warm up. She'd quite like to creep up onto Irene's lap.

When they have free time, she asks if Irene wants to play tag. Irene laughs and you can tell she likes children.

"Okay," she says and runs away. Hattie leaps after her. They charge between the tables where the others are sitting with books and puzzles.

Irene is hopeless at tag. "Tag! Tag! Tag!" Hattie calls out.

Irene has apricot tights on and she sighs about how unfit she is. "Gosh, you're good at this," she says.

Hattie is happy. "Shall you chase me now?" she says. Irene puffs and shakes her head. She understands that she could never in her whole life catch

Hattie, not even if Hattie was on crutches.

So they play a little more with Hattie chasing Irene. She gets easier and easier to catch. Her tights are completely sweaty. Hattie is ruthless and takes advantage of Irene when she stumbles or tries to rest for a moment. "Tag! Tag! Tag!"

Irene wipes her face. "Gosh, you are quick," she puffs. "I have to go to the bathroom."

She goes to the bathroom and locks herself in. Hattie is impatient. "Are you ready yet?" she calls. Irene laughs behind the door. Then Hattie understands!

"You're hiding!" she shouts and grabs the door handle. "Come out!"

Irene just laughs.

Hattie looks at the lock. It has a little spike sticking out. If she manages to turn it around, the door will open. But her fingers can't get a grip on it. Hattie runs away and grabs a pair of scissors with orange plastic handles.

With the scissors she gets hold of the little spike. She turns it around and throws open the door. "HA HA!" she says, pointing.

Irene is sitting there, pushing hard. There comes a plop!

"Close the door!" she yells furiously. "Can't a person even have a moment's peace in the toilet? What's this stupidity?"

Hattie closes the door with shaking hands and goes to sit on a stool. She feels as if she wants to cry. Grown-ups can be so unpredictable. In a second Irene has switched from being a cute round lady to a shrieking witch. Abracadabra.

She stays on the stool and stares at the wall till Church Children's Hour is over. Then she runs off without looking back.

"Goodbye, Hattie!" Irene calls, but Hattie doesn't answer. She flies out to the blue car where her mother is sitting waiting.

"It was boring," she says as she hops in. She's not going to say anything about Irene and the toilet.

Her mother starts the car and soon they're humming over the hills.

When they get home her father is happy that Hattie wants to stop going to the Church Children's Hour. "I told you it would be ridiculous," he says.

"Mmm," Hattie agrees. She pushes the green note from the Church Children's Hour to the bottom of the wastepaper basket.

THE
CLOWN

Hattie doesn't have long to be upset about Irene because the next day at school she hears something wonderful. The whole class will be going to the swimming pool in town to learn how to swim!

But the day before they go, the teacher says that at the swimming pool anyone with warts on their feet must wear swimming bootees so they don't give them to others.

Swimming bootees are ugly little shoes made of nylon and rubber. Hattie has never seen anyone swim with bootees…

Hattie has at least ten warts on her right foot. When she hears about the bootees she'd rather forget about swimming and stay home. But she's not allowed. Everyone must swim, the teacher says.

That evening Mama finds her swimming bag. She puts in the green bathing suit, a towel with Garfield the cat on it and one swimming bootee. Hattie will only wear one in the pool because she only has warts on one foot. One swimming bootee is almost worse than two. Only clowns go around with one shoe on.

At the pool she runs out and quickly jumps into the water so no one will see the bootee.

A swimming coach stands on the side giving the class instructions. She hops onto the stand and pedals her legs. The children are supposed to copy. It's much slower jumping around in water than it is up on the side, and soon everyone has tired muscles. Then the coach explains that they should go for a swimming badge.

She shows them a poster with pictures of all the badges. Hattie looks carefully at each one. Then she decides. She'll try for the Silver Frog.

To get the Silver Frog you have to swim to the first mark, tread water, and float for a while. The swimming coach walks alongside, checking.

So far, it's all going well. The last test is to collect a little plastic thing from the bottom of the pool.

Hattie has to put her head under water and dive down, taking her body, the bootee and the whole shebang.

The coach claps her hands. "Off you go!" she calls.

Hattie takes a deep breath and puts her head under, expecting to sink down.

It doesn't happen. She presses her whole body but she gets nowhere. She just lies floundering.

She lifts her head up again to breathe. The coach shakes her head. "You have to go down," she says.

"But how?" calls Hattie, rubbing the chlorine water from her eyes. "I just stop!"

"Just dive down," the coach urges, holding her arms out like a diver.

Hattie tries again. But it's like throwing yourself against a wall. She bobs like a cork on the surface, getting nowhere near the bottom. The plastic thing wobbles at her feet.

"You'll have to practice a little," says the coach. "Next time you might be able to try again."

Next time! Hattie sees stretching ahead a lifetime in swimming bootees. That can't happen! She has to get the Silver Frog now so swimming lessons will be over and done with.

The teacher bounds over and the swimming coach starts to explain that unfortunately Hattie hasn't succeeded with the diving for plastic test.

"Oh, that's a shame," says the teacher.

They're so busy with their conversation that they don't look at Hattie in the swimming pool. She gropes about with her foot, then she feels the plastic thing beneath her rubber sole. But she can't get a grip with the swimming bootee. She tries with her left foot instead. At last! Her toes pinch the plastic thing. Agile as an orangutan she lifts her foot. "I got it! I got it!" she shouts.

The teacher and the swimming coach look. They don't seem impressed. "I think you cheated." The coach looks almost sad. The teacher tugs his beard thoughtfully.

Hattie doesn't get the Silver Frog. The swimming bootee goes *claff-claff* as she heads to the shower. Now she's a cheat again, just like in Matt's Wood. But this time it's almost worse. This time she's a cheat in a clown shoe.

Soon Hattie goes with her mother and father to the hospital in town. The warts are going to be removed because Hattie has decided she'll never splash around again with a bootee on in the swimming pool. She sits in the back seat in despair.

Outside the snow is finally gone. Daisies stick up through the old faded grass and the ditches are full of yellow. The sun finds its way into the car where it's lovely and warm.

At the hospital she has to take off her sock and lie on a plastic sheet. The doctor takes out a sharp needle with the medicine that will numb her foot. Hattie tenses up...

And then comes the first prick. She wails like a police siren and tears pour from her eyes. Her parents look despairingly at her. "We'll buy you treats," her mother squeaks, patting her hand.

The doctor pricks again. Hattie kicks and flails.

"There, there," her mother comforts her. "Only a few to go."

The doctor pricks and pricks. Hattie yells and yells. And at last all feeling disappears. Her whole foot feels like a smooth custard.

The doctor wipes the sweat from his forehead. He's never had to deal with such a wild patient.

"Now then," he says, and rolls up his sleeves. It's just as well Hattie has such a lot of painkiller in her foot, because something worse is about to happen. The warts will be burnt off with a red-hot iron!

Hattie doesn't feel a thing. It just smells a little burnt, like when Mama's stew boils over on the stove.

But when it's over and Hattie thinks everything is a-okay again, the worst happens. The foot has to be bound up in a long bandage so Hattie can't put on her normal sneaker. The bandage means there's a thick white lump at the end of her leg. Mama is prepared for this. She's been to see Hattie's cousin, who's bigger than Hattie, and borrowed a pair of loafers!

A loafer is the worst. It's like a little prince's shoe in leather with a flat sole and tassles that sit and flap on the tongue. Hattie wants to die. A loafer is a million times worse than a clown shoe. When they go out to the car, Hattie's feet go *slap, clack, slap, clack, slap, clack*. One foot in a sneaker and the other in the ugly loafer.

On the way home they stop to buy treats. Nothing tastes good. All Hattie can think about is her ugly

clump-foot and the terrible little prince shoe.

But after a few days the bandage comes off and Hattie's cousin gets his shoe back. Soon it's time to go to the swimming pool again.

Hattie sits on the bus into town, enjoying it. In the swimming bag are only her bathing suit and the Garfield towel, no clown shoe.

After warming up, everyone is going to try for their badge again. Hattie swims to the first mark, treads water and floats.

Then it's time. The swimming coach throws in the plastic thing. "Off you go!" she calls. "Dive!"

Hattie dives. She flips her legs like an otter and sweeps with her arms. She reaches for the bottom… And she feels the thing in her hand! She bursts up, spraying water.

"I got it!"

The swimming coach claps her hands. "Ha ha!" she laughs. "That wasn't so hard, was it?"

Hattie jumps and jumps and jumps. She is the Silver Frog!

HAPPY EASTER

Once spring has started to show itself, everything happens fast. Soon there are blue anemones among the old leaves beneath the lilac hedge. The earth starts to crawl and tingle with newly woken life. Poof! Her mother's gardens turn yellow. The daffodils have appeared. Easter is here.

Hattie has been making paintings for several days now. She's done roosters, hens, hares, chickens and patterned eggs. Now it's Maundy Thursday, when everyone dresses up as witches.

Hattie finds some fun clothes in her mother's wardrobe. There's a skirt with one pocket and an old knitted cardigan. She takes a coffee pot from the kitchen. She folds up all her drawings into Easter letters. When she has painted her cheeks red,

off she goes. She's on the lookout for treats!

Out on the road sits Havana the cat, blinking at the sun-shiny puddles. Havana would make a perfect witch's cat. She could sit on Hattie's shoulder and hiss.

"Come!" calls Hattie.

Havana runs off to the stable to hiss at the sheep instead. She doesn't like sugar. But Hattie's looking forward to something sweet.

All her letters are in the skirt pocket. Twenty. She peers over at the little cottage where Alf lives. His digger is parked outside the door. That means he's home. Hattie goes over as fast as her boots will take her. She's soon there.

Alf has brown hair and a big nose. When he sees Hattie holding out an Easter letter, he's surprised. "Well, well, what a lovely little woman." He opens the letter and admires it. "And such a good drawing!"

Hattie smiles and waits. Alf tries to smile back. "Think," he mumbles and scratches his neck. "I'd completely forgotten that it's Maundy Thursday today. And I don't have any treats here…" He glances regretfully at Hattie.

Hattie feels how the corners of her mouth want to go down to her ankles, but she tightens her cheeks and keeps smiling.

Alf lights up. "Perhaps you'd like a cracker?" he says. Off he goes into the cottage. Soon he's back with a dry little cracker in his hand.

Hattie thanks him and accepts it. She says "Happy Easter" to Alf and leaves.

Alf is the only one who lives nearby. To reach any other houses she has to go quite far. But Hattie still has many lovely letters in her pocket and she longs to have just a few treats in her coffee pot. So she decides to carry on.

The boots clump and the sun warms her neck. Just before the road turns a big corner, there's a run-down old house with a tin roof. Hattie stops to look. She knows who lives in it. A drug addict. He has a cat that sits and caterwauls in the tree at night. She swallows a few times and straightens her back. The house looks dark. She takes a couple of steps onto the unkempt lawn, but then changes her mind and runs quickly out to the road again. When she thinks about it, Hattie doesn't think a drug addict is the sort of person to sit at home with a bucket of treats on Maundy Thursday, waiting for Easter witches.

She goes on walking in the mild spring breeze. The trees are budding and green. On every branch are small birds who are happy that the cold is over. They chatter and chirp so much that the forest sounds like a jungle.

Hattie plans to go to the summer houses. They're along the road past the big hill. But before Hattie gets there, she has to pass a brown house. In it lives a man who Papa says has a different kind of brain. Papa usually talks to him when they happen to meet. Not Hattie. She finds the man a bit strange. Sometimes she sees him standing and digging up the road with a spade. He makes a little hole and then he fills it in again. Hattie goes past without knocking.

The long hill is steep and it's hard to keep going. Hattie is out of breath when she reaches the top. Now she can see the little collection of summer houses. She runs the last bit.

When she arrives everything feels spooky. In the

tangled flowerbeds are brown, dry plants left from summer. There are rotten apples on the grass.

Slowly, slowly she creeps into one of the gardens. She knocks carefully at a door. No one comes to open it. Through the window she can see dead flies lying with their legs in the air. The summer visitors haven't come yet.

With heavy steps she goes back to the road. She still has nineteen letters left and zero houses to go to. A single cracker rattles in the coffee pot. Her bottom lip trembles. Stupid people. Stupid road, with no one living on it. Stupid summer visitors! It's fine to come flying in in June, but when it's Easter they're all sitting inside in town. Probably filling their stomachs with sugar as well.

With wet eyes, Hattie runs down the long hill the whole way home. They'll get it, she thinks. They sure will get it. Her head is boiling with ideas of revenge.

She takes the felt pens and closes the door to her room. Then she chooses her pens. It's always hard to find one that's the right shade for skin. In the end she chooses the pink one and she unfolds all the letters again.

Then Hattie starts to write down every bad word she's ever heard, sometimes with different spellings because she's not sure. All around the roosters, the hens, the chickens and the hares, she adds words in capital letters and with exclamation marks.

She puts her letters back in her pocket and off she goes again. The sun is lower in the sky. Soon it will disappear behind the fir trees, far away on the horizon.

At the summer houses she puts an Easter letter in every mailbox. Sometimes she even puts in two because otherwise she won't get rid of them all. When her pocket is empty, she quickly runs home. Laughter bubbles in her stomach. Oh, how she'd love to see the faces of all the summer guests when they open their mailboxes in June.

But when she comes inside and empties the coffee pot onto the kitchen table, she feels her heart grow heavy again. Out rolls the little cracker and it lies there tired and pathetic on the table. It's two whole days until Easter, when Hattie can look for Easter eggs. Tears prick her eyelids and her throat hurts from the hard lump in it.

Her mother rushes down from upstairs. "How did it go?" she chirps.

Hattie cries. "A cracker."

Her mother looks forlornly at the cracker. She puts her head to one side. "Poor little witch," she comforts her.

Then she goes to the kitchen cupboard and reaches up high. She pulls down a thick paper bag with red stripes. "It can't hurt to have a little something in advance," she says, and she puts a fistful of chocolate buttons, jelly snakes and sour balls in a bowl. Hattie takes the bowl, her eyes enormous. "You've deserved it," says Mama. "You made so many fine Easter letters."

Hattie lights up like the spring sun. "Thank you, Mama!"

NEW PET

The weather has warmed up properly. Hattie's mother finds the outdoor furniture and Hattie borrows a few things from the kitchen to use for mudpies. The hens, who have been sitting and sighing in the henhouse all winter, go out and forage all day long.

Papa builds a green seesaw for Hattie. It's lovely. The only trouble is that Hattie doesn't have anyone to seesaw with, because she still lives next door to no one. And Linda lives a whole mile away. Her parents never have time to drive her there.

The seesaw stays on the lawn, its paint flaking. It's so tempting for Papa's turkey that he can't help sneaking out of the woodshed to sit on it. And along comes the fox and eats him up! Hattie has escaped with her life. How terrifying if she'd been the one sitting on the seesaw!

Papa sweeps up the few feathers left from the turkey. "Poor old bird," he says, looking at the ground. He's always sad when animals get hurt.

In school one day Karin has something bulging in her pocket. Several times in class she peeps secretively down at it. By break time Hattie and Linda are so curious they're almost bursting.

"What have you got in there?" asks Hattie out in the school yard.

Karin smiles. "I'll show you." She pulls a pointy shell from her pocket. And from the pointy shell, a bony little crab crawls out.

"A crab!" Hattie cries.

"A hermit crab," Karin corrects her. "It's mine. I was given it."

Hattie is almost dizzy with love. For the whole day she can't think of anything apart from how badly she wants a crab.

When she comes home in the afternoon, she tells about Karin's pet.

Papa looks crestfallen. "She had it in her pocket?" He looks as if he might cry.

"Yes," Hattie squeaks.

Papa shakes his head and leaves the room.

Hattie follows. "Can I have a crab too?" she asks in her nicest voice.

Papa sits on the steps and bites his lip. "You can't keep animals like that in captivity," he says.

But then Hattie crosses her arms. "You do!" she says. "Sheep and ducks and everything!"

He looks at her in surprise. Then he puts his chin in his hands to think.

"Pleeeease," Hattie nags him.

Papa sits for a moment longer. Then he gets up. "I know what you can have," he says.

In the kitchen he takes out the biggest mixing bowl. Then he puts on his boots and opens the door. Hattie jumps into her boots too.

Soon they're tramping over the fields. In the distance Hattie can see the stream wiggling around a couple of corners and disappearing into the forest. She dances about and hops up and down. "A crab," she yelps. "Are we going to fish for one in the stream?"

Her father strides on, not giving anything away. At the stream they skid down the steep bank. "It will be cold if you fall in," Papa warns her.

Hattie is very curious. "Will we pull up the crab in a bucket? Yes? Papa? Will we?"

Papa shakes his head. "There are none here," he says. "But I'll show you something else." He leans into a bunch of reeds and puts his hand in the water. Soon he has a big lump of jelly with black dots in it. He puts that in the bowl and fills it with water.

"What's that stuff?" Hattie asks.

"Spawn," he says. "Soon it'll hatch into tadpoles. You can have them until they turn into frogs."

Hattie is radiantly happy about her new pets. After a couple of days the spawn hatches. The bowl is full of tiny baby tadpoles that swim around and splash as they play. She sits on the bench watching them.

"Can't we keep them when they become frogs?" she begs, but her father says no. Frogs don't want to live in a mixing bowl, he is sure. When the tadpoles are fully grown they have to be taken back to the stream. Hattie hopes that will take a long, long time.

The tadpoles can eat fish food, which her father

buys in town when he goes to the newspaper to talk about his articles. The food comes in small flakes. It smells of old fish and rotten seaweed. Hattie holds her breath every time she opens the jar. Poor tadpoles who have to eat such horrible flakes!

One day she opens the fridge to see if there's something nicer to offer them. At once she sees a lovely red carton. Cream is one of the nicest things there is, Hattie thinks. She could drink a bucket of it every day.

When her father comes in she asks, "Shall I feed the tadpoles a little bit of cream?"

Papa shakes his head hard. "No-oo." He explains earnestly that tadpoles do not like cream. They only like horrible flakes. Then he puts on his hat and disappears out to feed the sheep.

Hattie looks at her small pets. They look thin and wasted. You can clearly see how much they want to eat cream!

She opens the fridge again and reaches for the carton. She knows that the tadpoles will lick up the whole lot in a second. Then they'll never want to go back to the stream but rather stay with lovely Hattie who gives them cream.

Splosh! She pours in a splash and looks into the bowl... Right away, something seems wrong. The cream spreads quickly like a toxic cloud of exhaust, and the tadpoles flee for their lives! Hattie takes a big breath. "Papaaaa!"

Her father comes running. "No, no, no, no!" he says, rushing to the bench.

Then he has to take the bowl straight back to the stream because otherwise the tadpoles won't survive for more than ten minutes. Hattie stands at the bench watching him disappear over the field. Now she doesn't have tadpoles any more. All she has is a big jar of fishflakes.

HAPPY SUMMER

Karin doesn't have a pet any more either. Her crab was so stressed from being in her pocket that it died. Karin wears a black sorrow band around her head at school. If anyone happens to mention anything to do with crabs, she puts her head in her hands and howls.

The teacher sighs. "Try to be quiet now," he says. "We need to choose our songs for the end of year."

Soon it will be the last day of school. They're going to sing in church and anyone is welcome to come and listen. Hattie knows that her parents are planning to come.

The class has to vote for two songs. Anyone with a suggestion can put their hand up. The teacher will write them on the board.

"Away you go," he chirps.

Many hands go up and the teacher points. "Richard."

Richard puts his hand down. "*Rönnerdahl!*"

The whole class sighs at once. All the hands go down.

"I was going to say that," Karin complains.

The teacher looks displeased. He tugs his beard. Then he shakes his head. "Think of some others," he says, looking for more hands.

There are cries of protest. The children shout so much, the teacher has to cover his ears. "Quiet!" he calls. "You can't have the *Rönnerdahl!*"

Then he explains why. The song of Rönnerdahl happens to have been written by a man called Evert Taube. And Taube happens to have written many rude songs. The teacher knows he'll be disgraced for eternity if they sing that sort of song in church.

"It can be interpreted rudely," he says. "Choose another one."

Linda puts up her hand. The teacher's face lights up. "Yes?"

"*Take Me to the Sea*," says Linda.

"Yesss!" everyone shouts. "Let's have that one!"

"Not that one," squeaks the teacher. "That one's even worse. It's about wine and women and all kinds of things."

"Yesss!" cries the class. "*Take Me to the Sea!*"

The teacher gives them a wild look. Then he walks purposefully to the blackboard. He writes *Rönnerdahl*. He stands in front of it for a moment, thinking. Then he lifts his hand and writes *Now Spring Is Come*.

He turns around and looks at them sternly. "So," he says. "You've voted for one and I've voted for one. Now we'll start rehearsing."

Everyone in the class sings as loudly as they can while the teacher tinkles on the piano. When they've finished for the day, he stands up and puts a finger in the air. "I have something important to tell you," he says. "No one will put their hands together and clap when we've finished our singing at the end of year, because it's absolutely forbidden to clap in church. It's important," he says again. "So if there's anyone at home who doesn't know about it being forbidden you must tell them. Okay?"

"Okay!" they all cry. Now they can go home.

The same day, Hattie goes with her mother to town. They're going to buy best clothes to wear for the last day of school. Hattie chooses a white skirt with flounces and a white jacket with diamonds on the collar. She's never seen anything more beautiful. "Can I wear it to school tomorrow?" she asks.

But she can't.

"You have to wait for end of school," says her mother. "Otherwise you take the fun out of it."

Hattie can't understand that. If your clothes are beautiful, it's best to wear them as much as you can! At least she knows she'll feel good on the last day.

"Pleeeease," she says. And she goes on so much that her mother wants to take the clothes back to the shop. That stops Hattie's nagging.

The skirt and the jacket stay at home on the cane chair and are temptingly beautiful. Every morning Hattie pats the flounces and yearns. Then she puts on her old jeans as usual. Just until...

End of school! Now the mornings are warm and light. The sun has been awake for a long time when Hattie hops out of bed and runs over to the cane chair. In the garden the peonies bob on their sturdy stalks and birds chirp in all the bushes.

Hattie struggles to eat her breakfast sandwich and milk. She's not at all hungry. All she wants is to finish school.

"It's rude to clap your hands in church," she says.

"That's right," her mother replies.

Papa says nothing. He frowns and looks at his yogurt.

Mama looks suspiciously at him. "Very rude," she says.

"Hrm," Papa mutters.

Then all three of them go to Hardemo in the blue car. They go over the hills and past the green fields. And then they come to the school, as always. But now someone has decorated the entrance with birch boughs and over the doorway is a banner. *Happy summer!* it says. It looks festive.

In the classroom they give the teacher a round glass candlestick. All the class put in money and Ellen's mother bought it in town. Hattie thinks the candlestick looks like a heap of mashed potato.

But the teacher is so happy he cries. He rubs his

hands over his tired, baggy eyes. The summer holidays will be good for him, too.

And off they march. The school and the church are next door to each other. They only have to go twenty steps over the parking area and they've arrived. First come the year sixes with the flag on a pole. Then come the year fives, then the fours, the threes, the twos and, last, Hattie's class. They're the smallest.

The priest talks for a long, long time. Hattie tries to listen but she's too nervous. Soon they'll go to the front and sing!

When it's time the teacher waves for them to stand up. Hattie's legs feel like boiled spaghetti. Imagine if she sings something wrong! She'll be mortified for the rest of her life.

They form rows in front of the altar. The teacher goes over to the piano on one side. He starts to play. Between two chords he holds up one hand, which means they should start singing. Hattie is alert. She roars the first line of the song.

At first she almost faints because no one else is singing. But by the second line Karin has begun to chirp and soon the whole class is bawling the last line loudly. "Cowslip, saxifrage, catsfoot…"

Hattie sniggers. Linda usually sings "catspoop…" She's standing next to Hattie in a pale blue dress. She's as sweet as ever. And Hattie can tell she's also giggling.

After that they sing *Now Spring Is Come*. It all goes very well. Hattie doesn't say the wrong word a single time. When they've finished they're allowed to curtsey or bow, then they're supposed to go back to their seats and sit down.

But something terrible happens. Someone claps! Hattie stares at the pews.

Papa! His hands are high in the air and he's clapping as hard as he can. "Bravo!" he calls. Everyone in church stares at him. Mama is flushed.

Then someone else is clapping! Hattie turns around. It's the priest! He smiles. The teacher looks confused. But now several people are clapping and soon the church is thundering with applause. Then the teacher perks up and runs to the front to take a bow. The class bow and curtsey several times and the teacher beams with pride. They've been a success! Happy summer!

BEAUTIFUL FLOWERS

Now all the summer visitors turn up. Hattie feels a little nervous in case they find out who put such beautiful Easter letters in their mailboxes. There are no other naughty children around here…

She runs over in her clogs. Maybe she can take some of the letters back before it's too late.

She gets as far as the big corner when she stops and looks down into the ditch. All the flowers are growing there now, crinkly little birdsfoot, flouncy red clover and violet granny bonnets. Hattie knows that her mother loves flowers. She'll pick a bunch to surprise her with!

The bunch grows slowly bigger. It's as scrawny as a piece of string and the granny bonnets sprawl in all directions. The dandelions in the ditch also want to be picked but they can't be, they're too ugly. Hattie wanders on, further and further from the house.

Up by the summer houses she looks inside some of the mailboxes. She has to be careful because mailboxes always have earwigs running around in them. Hattie has heard that earwigs run into people's ears and settle there. Then they build nests and won't come out. Ugh!

She can't see any earwigs. No Easter letters either. They've probably blown away, she thinks. Or they might have crumpled up and disappeared.

Relieved, she turns around and heads for home. The sun is shining and the grass tickles her legs. Then she stops short, her mouth open.

In the ditch, just a bit away, is a whole jungle of flowers! Not stumpy little clovers, pathetic granny bonnets or scraggly old birdsfoot. These are completely different. The flowers reach Hattie's neck and look like pink and violet spires. She's never seen anything growing so proudly in a ditch, as wild as dandelions. And no one has come to pick them! She throws away her tatty bunch and starts a new one.

The air hums. The flowers are hard to pick. Hattie has to tug and pull. Mama will love these; she'll pick them all. The bunch grows quickly. Soon she can't hold all the thick stems in one hand. She has to hug the flowers and carry them like a doll in her arms. She avoids a bee and goes on picking. The ditch is full of flowers. And bees.

After a long time Hattie has picked every single flower. Only lank grass stalks are left in the ditch. Then she goes home.

She can hardly see the road for the bushy bunch in her arms. The pink and violet spires tickle her face. Her mother will be so happy, Hattie thinks, as she quickens her pace.

Soon she's crunching over the gravel in front of the red house. She scurries up the steps and into the kitchen where her mother is standing.

"Aha, there you are," she says when she sees Hattie.

Hattie is as radiant as the sun. Her mother is beaming like...a careful sun.

"I wondered when you might come," she says. "Wanda called."

So what? Hattie has flowers! "These are for you, Mama," she shouts, thrusting out the bunch.

"Oh, thanks." Mama takes them. "Yes, well, Wanda rang."

Hattie is disappointed. Mama isn't nearly as pleased as a person should be when they're given a bunch of seldom-seen most-beautiful flowers. She only wants to talk about Wanda.

Wanda comes to her little summer cottage every year when it gets warm. She's nice. Wanda often gives Hattie jars of honey because she has lots of beehives. She lives right next to where Hattie found all the flowers.

"She said that she saw through the window that you'd picked all her lupins, which she sowed on the property," says her mother, trying to smile.

Hattie stands there in silence, staring at the bunch of flowers. The spires are called lupins. Now she understands why no one else has picked them. Flowers someone has planted are not for picking. Her heart pounds in fear. Tears creep under her eyelids. Why didn't Wanda come out and say something when Hattie had only picked one or two flowers? Why did she sit there staring behind her curtains till it was too late? Now Hattie never wants to go back to the summer cottages. Wanda won't want to see her again either.

Her mother puts the lupins in a vase on the table. She takes a couple of steps back and looks at them. "They're beautiful, anyway," she says.

Beautiful? Hattie's never seen such ugly flowers in her whole life. Lupins make her feel sick.

When her mother has left the kitchen, Hattie takes the lupins and throws them on the compost heap. They lie there among the rotten potatoes and old onion tops.

On top of the compost heap is a single dandelion. She takes it and puts it in a vase. A dandelion is a thousand billion times more beautiful than lupins, thinks Hattie.

TO SUMMER PARADISE

Soon Hattie is going where you'll never see a glimmer of a dandelion. She's going on a summer trip.

Mama and Papa have booked it. The whole family is flying to an island called Rhodes, which is a Greek paradise. They have the tickets and now there's only one day to go.

Hattie's so happy that her legs hop all by themselves. She dances around the kitchen and her mother stands at the sink and laughs. Papa sits on the kitchen sofa with a map of Rhodes' black rocky terrain. He's planning excursions.

That evening when Hattie should be asleep, her bed feels about as comfortable as a slab of rock. The mattress seems to have mounded up, the covers twist and the pillow is lumpy. She'll never sleep!

She'll lie here awake with her eyes open till she grows old and dies! It's so light out in the sky.

Her parents are still up, running around and packing. On the floor in Hattie's room is a little suitcase. She's put everything into it. Bathing suit and skirt and sunglasses. For Snoopy she's packed a pair of tennis shorts and a pullover. When they fly he'll wear his cowboy costume.

He lies next to Hattie and looks her in the eyes. "Sleep now," he says. And then she goes to sleep.

But straight away she has to wake up again. They leave so early in the morning it's almost the middle of the night. Her mother and father put the suitcases in the blue car. Then Papa puts the key under the door mat because Alf next door will come and feed all the animals while they're away.

Hattie throws herself into the back seat and goes straight to sleep. When she wakes up they're already at the airport. They leave their suitcases at a desk and go to "the gate." The gate is what you call it.

Inside the cramped plane they each have a small seat. They fasten their seatbelts, Hattie clutches Snoopy tight, and next thing they're up and away!

Rhodes really is a paradise. The beach is right next to the hotel and they go there every day. The sand runs hot and tickly into your shoes. Papa is worried that Hattie will get webbed feet because she swims so much. Mama is worried that she'll turn into a brown biscuit because the sun's so fierce.

"Can't you swim in a T-shirt?" she begs.

But Hattie is never going to swim in anything but a bathing suit: no clown bootees and certainly no T-shirt.

"No," she says, and skips away when her mother tries to make her.

Mama frowns. Then she takes off her bikini top and sunbathes topless. She doesn't think it matters if she turns into a brown biscuit herself. She thinks that's good.

Someone who doesn't get brown is her father. He runs into the shade as soon as he gets a chance. On the beach he sits beneath an umbrella and he looks like a white seal in shirt and trousers.

"Phew, it's hot," he complains and runs his finger over the Rhodes map. "I'm going to hire a car."

And he does. He hires a cool sports jeep, without

a roof and with big tough tires. He's pleased. He's looked forward to this outing for ages.

Mama's pleased too. With her sunglasses on, she'll sit beside Hattie's father looking chic as they zoom around the island at high and dangerous speeds.

Hattie sits in the back seat and Snoopy sits beside her in his cowboy costume.

Vroom vroom! Papa accelerates and soon they're far from the tourist village. Now they're lurching through the beautiful rocks. Hattie is enjoying herself to the full. Snoopy too. He waves his cowboy hat at everyone they pass.

But after a while Hattie sees that Snoopy looks pale and faint. Sweat runs down his soft white forehead and his nose is dry. "Would you like to get changed?" she asks. Snoopy would.

Hattie rummages in the bag. She pulls out the pullover and continues to search. She takes out bikinis and watermelon, sandals and blow-up balls. But however deep she digs, she can't find his shorts. Snoopy looks at her in anguish.

Hattie suddenly realizes. The shorts must have blown away! Because the bag was open and her father has been driving like the wind! "STOPPP!" she cries.

Papa screeches to a stop. "What's the matter?" He gives her a worried look in the rear vision mirror.

"Snoopy's shorts have blown out of the car!"

"Just now?" asks her mother.

"No! I don't know! Some time. We have to go back!"

Mama and Papa squirm. They think it'll be hard to find the shorts because they've gone so far already. They'd rather keep going.

Hattie panics. Snoopy has no other shorts. He'll have to go around in his leather trousers the whole holiday. Or even worse, naked! Tears stream from her eyes. Her parents scratch their heads. Hattie cries even harder and soon Snoopy is crying too. He howls like a wolf. In the end Papa turns the car around and back they go.

Now he doesn't drive like a tough guy at racing speed. Now he has to creep along like a snail while Hattie looks right and left for Snoopy's shorts.

Mama takes off her sunglasses. She doesn't look at all chic any more. She just looks bored.

Papa sighs. "Can you see them?" he asks.

"No! Don't drive so fast!" Hattie shrieks back.

The whole day they putter along in the rugged rental jeep looking for Snoopy's shorts. Except Papa calls them Snoopy's "underpants." Hattie feels offended. Snoopy does too. Papa suggests Snoopy could borrow Mama's bikini bottoms instead of his lost shorts. Mama is offended.

They never find the shorts. Night comes and the jeep has to go back to the rental company. They don't rent another car on the holiday. They go to the beach instead and Papa sits under the umbrella and pants in the heat. The map of Rhodes' dangerous rocky terrain is left rolled up in the hotel room.

A NEW YEAR

When they get back to Sweden, Papa races up to his room. He writes a funny article for the newspaper about how crazy it was when Hattie made them spend a whole day on Rhodes looking for underpants. Hattie thinks she'll die and has to go secretly to her room and say a prayer: "Dear God, please let no one at school read the newspaper."

But God has more important things to think about than Hattie. When school begins the whole class thinks it's hilarious that she's so interested in underpants. Underpants fanatic!

Now the apples are hanging off the tree in the school yard. There are pears too. Everyone eats them and gets a sore stomach. Hattie included.

The teacher seems to be well again. "Welcome,"

he says, "to a new year at Hardemo."

Then they have to write about what they've done in the summer. Hattie writes so much her pen is on fire. She skips over the bit about the underpants, but it still ends up being several pages long.

The teacher smiles as she reads it aloud up at the blackboard.

"Clever," he says. "Rich in content."

Linda hasn't been anywhere, Hattie knows. But when it's time for her to read aloud, she scampers up to the blackboard and squints at Hattie with glittering eyes.

Then she reads two pages about how she's been to Africa chasing elephants this summer. Hattie laughs so hard she thinks her head will fall off. And suddenly the teacher looks a little, just a little bit, tired again.

It's the first day of school. Just like one year ago. Except not really. Everything is actually completely different.

HELLO FRIDA NILSSON

Describe yourself in three words.
Funny, stubborn, brown-haired.

Best animal, food, book?
Basset hound, fresh crayfish, Pelle Holm's
Bevingade Ord (a book of classic quotes).

Describe a really good day.
I write half a chapter I'm really pleased with, sit
for a while on the steps, cook, drink a little wine.

What makes you happy?
The woods.

What makes you sad?
Stories about people and animals in the world
who are mistreated.

Why do you write books?
To think about something else for a while,
and to find out if it has a happy ending.

How do you get ideas for your books?
Sources of inspiration?
When my mother and father talk about how
things were in the past.

Describe a typical writing day.
I start early before breakfast, drink five cups of coffee up to lunch, then I finish at two or three.

What is the most fun thing about writing books?
When you think of something that makes the story much better.

And the hardest?
When you write a paragraph five times without it turning out the way it should.

Which character from one of your own books would you choose to take with you on a long journey?
Probably Siri from *The Ice Sea Pirates*—she is used to travelling and can handle most things.

Photo © Ellinor Collin

This edition first published in 2020 by Gecko Press
PO Box 9335, Wellington 6141, New Zealand
info@geckopress.com

English-language edition © Gecko Press Ltd 2020
Translation © Julia Marshall 2020

Original title: Hedvig!
Text © Frida Nilsson and Natur & Kultur, Stockholm 2005
Illustrations © Stina Wirsén and Natur & Kultur, Sotckholm 2005
English edition published in agreement with Koja Agency

Distributed in the United States and Canada by Lerner Publishing Group
lernerbooks.com
Distributed in the United Kingdom by Bounce Sales and Marketing
bouncemarketing.co.uk
Distributed in Australia and New Zealand by Walker Books Australia
walkerbooks.com.au

The cost of this translation was defrayed by a subsidy from the
Swedish Arts Council, gratefully acknowledged.

Edited by Penelope Todd
Design and typesetting by Vida & Luke Kelly
Printed in China by Everbest Printing Co. Ltd,
an accredited ISO 14001 & FSC-certified printer

ISBN hardback: 978-1-776572-70-0 (USA)
ISBN paperback: 978-1-776572-71-7
Ebook available

For more curiously good books, visit geckopress.com